John Wetherbee

Shadows

John Wetherbee

Shadows

ISBN/EAN: 9783337423865

Printed in Europe, USA, Canada, Australia, Japan

Cover: Foto ©Andreas Hilbeck / pixelio.de

More available books at **www.hansebooks.com**

"SHADOWS:"

BEING

A FAMILIAR PRESENTATION

OF

THOUGHTS AND EXPERIENCES

IN

SPIRITUAL MATTERS,

WITH

ILLUSTRATIVE NARRATIONS.

BY

JOHN WETHERBEE.

" Concerning those spiritual beings which
' Walk the earth
Unseen, both when we wake and when we sleep.'
Are there, indeed, such beings?   Is this space between us and the
Deity filled up by innumerable orders of spiritual beings?"—*W. Irving.*

◆◆◆

BOSTON:
COLBY & RICH, PUBLISHERS,
Corner Bosworth and Province Sts.
1885.

DEDICATION.

To Louise,

The wife of my youth, who is also my wife and inspirer now in my maturity. How much during the past two or three decades have we together thought over these once strange, but now, by long association, familiar realities? When our first-born passed into the world of silence, where she is now,—the unseen but not an unperceived member of our otherwise unbroken family,—how sweet to have found the "Gates Ajar," so that we both realized that, though invisible, she was not absent,—when with fear, but hopefully, we wrote, inspired by our grief :—

> Oh, philosophy! destroy not the charm
>   That cheers thus our hours of sadness;
> Dissolve not the spell, if 't is but a dream,
>   That changes our sorrow to gladness.
>
> These little soft raps we now and then hear
>   I feel are the voice of my daughter;
> They seem to be saying: " Dear mother, I 'm here,"
>   Though they sound like the dropping of water.
>
> Our two little boys when they hear these raps,
>   Too young, like us, to have missed her,
> Look up with a smile, and say: " Do you hear
>   The voice of our dear little sister?"

Neither philosophy nor experience has disturbed the current of our happy belief; and while our loved little one has grown into womanhood in the land of souls, the inspiring fact has strengthened in us with our years. I have felt like saying this much, and to say also that this book is due to you, for I doubt if I would have put my thoughts into this form but for your persuasion from appreciation of my written words and of me; so to you, my beloved, the well-preserved mother of our Hattie, at an age when sentiment is apt to have gone into eclipse,— happily not in our case, —I dedicate these " SHADOWS " to you, feeling assured that in the alembic of your own mind and heart they will show up both as summer and sunshine.   J. W.

PREFACE.

I HAVE been rather arbitrary in calling these pages "SHADOWS," for there is nothing particularly shadowy in them, except that the subject in many minds is suggestive of the shadowy. The following colloquy, which lately occurred, as given below, will explain its title as well as in any other way, if an explanation is of any consequence : —

Mr. Shadows was seated, pen in hand, at his writing table, when his friend, Mr. Boulder Scratches, entered the room, and, seeing the situation, said: "Well, Shadows, what are you at now ?" "I have a book inside of me," said he, or the matter of one, and I havé made up my mind to make it manifest in the form." "On what subject?" said Scratches; or, I need not ask that, but what is the special point in Spiritualism to be treated, or what is the name or title of the book to be ?" " I do not know myself yet," said Shadows ; there is time enough for a name before it will be ready for the printer." Scratches said : "When I write anything, I start with a title." " I never do," said Shadows ; but now you have spoken of it, and are not a novice in book-making, I think a name would help me some. I wish I had one cut and dried, and adapted to my thought." "Why do n't you name it after yourself," said he ; your name and Spiritual-

5

ism seem to be suggestive of each other. '*Come like shadows, so depart,*'" he said, quoting from Macbeth, — the low or deep voice in which he spoke it struck him favorably, and he said: "I think I will; my name or your name, 'Shadows, or 'Scratches,' — I do n't know but I like 'Scratches' the better, — but as you may wish some day to use 'Scratches,' I guess I will christen mine 'SHADOWS.'"

The endeavor has been in these chapters, or, as now called, Shadows, *first*, that each one should be a finished one of itself, using the word finish in rather a liberal sense,— that is, that each chapter should be a readable one, without any special connection with the other, and aiming at no logical or consecutive order, so that in reading them one can skip about without any confusion.

The endeavor has also been, in the matter presented, to make the chapters in their wholeness give the reason, without particularly saying so, why I am a Spiritualist, not that it is of any consequence to the public what I am, or in what I believe, but being rather a man of the world and of business, one who has touched current life actively, if not broadly, and who is not constitutionally a dreamer or a sentimentalist. In my retired or private social circle I am not thought to be one whose tendencies would be either religious or spiritual, but being, I trust, both, the chapters, or shadows, that compose this book, will explain the reason why, if it be a matter of interest to anyone.

The endeavor has also been to make this book a familiar presentation of the subject of modern Spiritualism to those whom it may concern, both among its exponents and among that wider world who feel interested in the subject, and wish it were true, and who, like myself, want the "bottom facts."

In what I have said I have aimed at simplicity, and I know I have been truthful. If I have used the personal pronoun too much for good taste, no one is more aware of it than I am, but it could not very well be avoided with what I had in contemplation. My apology then is my desire, by this familiar, confidential way of expressing myself, to be persuasive, or, at least, to command the attention of the thoughtful reader.

J. W.

CONTENTS.

CHAPTER XIX.
INDIAN-SPIRIT INFLUENCES.

CHAPTER XX.
A WAYSIDE SKETCH.

CHAPTER XXI.
MATTER AND SPIRIT.

CHAPTER XXII.
A PENUMBRAL SKETCH.

CHAPTER XXIII.
MATERIALIZATION.

CHAPTER XXIV.
CUI BONO ?

CHAPTER XXV.
PREVISION.

CHAPTER XXVI.
DETACHED THOUGHTS.

CHAPTER XXVII.
THE BOSTON OUTLOOK.

"A few years since I had a long conversation with a bishop, who is held in deservedly high reputation by the orthodox body of Christians to which he belongs. He introduced the subject of modern Spiritualism, and I asked him how he regarded its phenomena. He answered frankly and satisfactorily. He said that evidences of infidelity were multiplying among us; he lately heard a professor of Harvard College say that three-fourths of the scientific men of our day are unbelievers, and skepticism is beginning to intrude among the clergy. He told me that he himself, a few weeks before, had visited the death-bed of an aged brother in the ministry, a man who had devoted a long life with rare faithfulness to the duties of his profession. As they spoke of the evidences of Christianity, a shade of sadness passed over the dying man's face. 'Ah, bishop,' said he, 'the proof, the proof! If we only had it!'"—*R. D. Owen, in "Debatable Land."*

11

I.

INTRODUCTORY.

Giving in a familiar way the Genesis and the Exodus of these chapters, which the author has somewhat arbitrarily called "Shadows."

The writer trusts that what he may say in the way of introduction will be as much a part of the main argument of the book as if he had written it under some more definite heading. His intention or object can be better set forth in this way than in the several chapters that follow, saving superfluity, enabling him to better present the subject in its many points with simplicity and brevity.

If one writes, or rather publishes, a book, he should have something to say, and a motive for saying it. The writer thinks he has something to say on what he considers the most important subject for human consideration; and most thoughtful people will agree with him on that point, very likely, however, qualifying this superlative expression with an "*if*," saying, *if* there were anything definitely known about it. If the writer, by his long experience and investigation under great advantages, did not consider the qualifying *if* a superfluity, and that he

knew with about as much certainty the truth of this
somewhat transcendental subject as he did of things
in general that are considered by thoughtful, scholarly people as true and worthy of attention, he would
show his wisdom by remaining silent. Whether he
has anything to say, therefore, the production must
speak for itself. As for the motive he has for writing the book, he has many; the principal one is, he
has been persuaded that what he has to say is really
wanted, and deserves a hearing. In this connection,
by way of explanation, the following circumstance
will not be out of place: —

He will now more familiarly address the reader;
thinks he can come closer, and express himself better in a change from the third to the first person,
even at the expense of apparent egotism, for which
he asks pardon.

A very venerable minister, residing in the State of
New York, attracted by the fascinating subject of a
future life, began a correspondence with me. He
was much nearer his ninetieth than to his eightieth
year; had had a long, successful, and useful career;
had been for many years the settled minister over a
church of the liberal, or Unitarian, order. He had,
of course, in that capacity, performed the marriage
and the funeral services of his people and neighborhood during all that time. He had consoled the
mourners in their bereavement when death had
drafted from their midst the old or the young faces
of the family circles in his parish or town. I do not
know at what period these ministerial consolations

had become merely a form, his faith in a future life having gone into eclipse, and agnostic ideas had taken possession of his mind; but when he began his correspondence with me he had doubts of the future or continued existence of man after the death of the body, and on that account he had retired from his pulpit into a private, scholarly, thoughtful life.

Somebody had sent him an article that I had written, in which I had narrated an experience which, he said, "if true to the letter, would settle the question affirmatively in his mind," and he began the correspondence of which I have spoken, and which grew interesting to both of us. I found him so penetrating, acute, and mentally vigorous that I never dreamed of his being so old a man, as later I learned he was.

Now I will take the liberty of digressing just for a minute, following my impression, and, doing so, will be in keeping with my statement that, though this is an "Introduction," it is also something more than one. Thinking of this thoughtful old man leads me to say, in this episodical way, that mental activity in the line of hopeful thought is a great lengthener of human life,—occupation of one's mind on high matters, whether on the scientific plane or in the religious or the spiritual direction, so long as the pabulum is mentally nutritious, that is truthful, or seemingly so. I hope the reader will understand me when I say rational thought, for a man may be very earnest, very fluent, and very full of moral and religious ideas, based on what, in his own mind, he does not consider reasonable or true; no matter how sure he pretends to be of his premises, having scriptural endorsement and the whole army of Bible believers to sustain him, — that kind of truth which may in a man's heart seem untrue,— I do not offer as nutritious food or life-prolonging. A sure and happy future life, after the mortal one has ended, in one's mind, based on sensuous proof, or even on intuition, if it amounts to proof, is a lengthener of life in this world, and, all other things being equal both in a man's Genesis and his Exodus, it adds youthfulness also to his longevity. Let no one now quote the many exceptional instances to this bold statement, and mention, perhaps, Theodore Parker, who was really eighty when he was only fifty, and who on this theory was entitled to duration; nor many a poor, thoughtless, hard-working, and very ignorant person who outstays his threescore-and-ten a decade or two, for these are the exceptions. Statistics show that the studious and scholarly class outlast the laboring class in longevity. With the sensuous, proof that a man not only has a future beyond the dark valley, but one that is an extension of this life into the domain of the spiritual, as it becomes a matter of general acceptance, will add to human longevity.

Many things have already extended the average length of human life from what it was a hundred years ago,— sanitary attention, wisdom in living, better ventilation, and the principle of the survival of the fittest, carrying its momentum with it, have effected this improvement, which is a matter of fact,

now add to these important factors not only the hope
but the demonstration of the survival of the man
beyond the death of the body, then, when its belief
is as general as is the belief in the Copernican system, or as it is to those who constitute the body
politic of Spiritualism, it will add still more to the
years of human duration, and to its usefulness also,
for the face behind the mask is not supposed to be a
wrinkled one.

Returning now from this episode to our venerable
ex-minister, with whom, as has been stated, I have
had much correspondence,— whose earnest, vigorous
words have impressed me both with his command of
language, his logic, and his sincerity. I liked very
much his interrogatories, his incisive thrusts into my
statements, his desire for the "bottom facts." I think
he did me good, whether I relieved him from his
doubts or not. I really made no effort to convert
him. I never do to anyone; am making none now
in writing this book. To make converts, or the con-
version of anyone, is to me a matter of indifference.
I sometimes think the doctrine of election shows
itself in this matter, as it does in many others, as a
constitutional quality, so that the old orthodox point
may after all have had some natural basis of truth.
I simply gave this correspondent what, from my
point of view, appeared to be the truth regarding
modern Spiritualism, illustrating it from my experience.

I want it to be understood by all that I am a
Spiritualist from experience. I do not think I could

believe as I do on anyone's testimony. People are differently constituted; some believe more readily than others; some people are helped by their intuitions. Theodore Parker once said to me, speaking of "spiritual manifestations," that he needed no proofs of another life; if he had any doubts, it was of this life,—whether this world was a reality,—none at all of the other. Blessed are these men who are such born believers. They are the ones who in all ages have kept the sacred fire of hope alive and burning. The mass of mankind, particularly in this materialistic age, lack this inspiring intuition, and so need sensuous proof, and, without it, are without faith.

Our venerable minister says, in one of his letters, that if he had my experience, and knew that it was so, he would be a believer, and be happy. Sometimes he is afraid, he says, I am beguiled by others, or, perhaps, by my own desires. It is possible I am; I am only human, but I hardly think so; if I in any degree thought so, I would at once lay down my pen. I am as sure of my facts, in this line of thought, as I am of them in any other department of knowledge.

As I propose in the following chapters to give some of my experiences as well as some of my inferences and deductions, I am taking some liberty in this introductory chapter to impress upon the reader, as I did upon this minister, that I am dealing with positive facts, and not suppositions. I am sure there is a power, impulse, or force in nature not recognized as yet by science, or as something outside of the rec-

ognized domain of science; the best exoteric definition of it is *Psychic Force*. This power, or force, is
certainly intelligent, even if ultra human. It claims
to be a voice from "over the river" from departed
spirits; it claims to be from the loved and lost, from
those whose bodies are moldering in the grave,
assuring us mortals that they still live. This intelligent "*psychic force*" has never claimed to be anything else but a departed human being, in a single
instance, from the first manifestation in 1848 to the
present time. It probably never will. It looks to
me as if it was going, as the saying is, "to laugh
last," or best.

With the evidence I have, some of which I propose to present, I am obliged to take this "Psychic
Force's" word, and believe in dealing with it I am
dealing, not with the dead, but with those whose
mortal forms only are tenants of the world's sepul-
chers, but who are still living entities; I am obliged
to respect that claim, for I would stultify my understanding if I did not. I am aware that outside of
this mysterious source of information, this "spiritual
environment," that the subject suggests, is not
proved; so, in a sense, to assume it, is begging the
question; but if it be admitted as a verity, as the
Bible, and as poetry in general is authority for,
"that we are surrounded by a countless multitude of
witnesses," or, in the words of the poet, that

"The spiritual world
Lies all about us, and its avenues
Are open to the unseen feet of phantoms

> That come and go, and we perceive them not,
> Save by their influence."

That is, make the scriptural or sentimental idea a matter of fact, then one must explain the phenomena of modern Spiritualism as being what it claims to be, —the spirits of the departed, as poetically expressed in the following lines : —

> "There is a world of spirits fair
> All around us and unseen;
> And those whom we call 'dead' are there
> With all that erst on earth hath been."

As I believe in this spiritual environment, I believe the claim that in every case this "Psychic Force " makes, which it made eighteen hundred years ago, and which in the modern form it makes today. Perhaps the older affirmation will express the idea as well as any other,—so I will quote that, where John the Revelator, in the presence of the angel, which it seems was only a departed spirit, said (Rev. xix: 10): "And I fell at his feet to worship him. And he said unto me, See thou do it not: I am thy fellow-servant, and of thy brethren that have the testimony of Jesus: worship God."

I do not know anything in the whole realm of physics, or what are called real things, more surely than I know that there is this spiritual surrounding which is taught in the Bible, and taught by modern Spiritualism.

The human intellect, as Ernest Renan says, is infidel; it asks questions, and so it should; but the heart is the true believer; hence poetry bubbles out of it full of nutritious sentiment that ought to be true, and what the sensuous proof, through modern Spiritualism, makes literal and true. Here is one of its expressions; what a dreary world this would be if it were not a hope and a possibility: —

"Oh! Heaven is nearer than mortals think,
When they look with a trembling dread
At the misty future that stretches on
From the silent home of the dead."

In corresponding with this aged but strong-minded man, I found myself drawn to him, and though he was at that period of life that demonstration of this matter was soon to be in the order of nature, I felt moved to be very open and frank with him,—am astonished sometimes that I made the effort I did to justify my belief and to defend my perspicuity. Perhaps I was influenced to do so; knowing what I do, I am obliged to believe that there is this influence, or watchful supervision of the world of spirits on or over the affairs of every-day life. At any rate, writing, as I generally do, to be printed rather than for autographical correspondence, it was singular that I wrote this man so extensively as I did, and which, I trust, as I have said, has benefited both of us.

When I received his last letter, which only antedates this chapter a few days, it seemed to call for this, may I say, "diffusion of knowledge." If what I had written to him in this fugitive way seemed to him valuable enough to say, rather urgingly, that I ought to print it, and knowing his sincerity when he says in the last letter, to which I have referred: " I am not well, and so cannot answer your last, but my main object in this is to make a suggestion, and it is this: that you gather what you have written to me on this subject, including some of your experiences from which you so freely draft, into a book, which would be of a very interesting and readable character, and just what thoughtful people want to read. Is not this a suggestion worthy of your serious thought? I have not less than fourteen articles from you that, of themselves, would make an attractive volume. Your letters to me on the subject are very valuable, and are worthy of a more extended perusal."

It would seem, then, by a person competent to judge, that some of my thoughts, experiences, and hurried reflections have a value. I have had other similar suggestions from various sources. A letter from Alabama, just received, written in a very persuasive manner, " to put some of my thoughts into a book form on this subject, in which we are all so interested, and know so little about, and I feel, whenever I read anything of yours, I am getting an honest and intelligent view of the subject from your standpoint." These letters, coming so together, seemed to say to me that I had better venture to do so. Perhaps the intimation to do so dates higher than the State of New York, or of Alabama, or other mundane localities. We do not always know the sources of our inspiration. I am inclined to think our thoughts and acts, great and small, are the result of influences from the world of spirits, so near and yet so remote. It seems to be asking the reader to take it for granted that the claim is proved before I begin my story, so I will close this preliminary chapter, it having done its work by embodying the reasons for issuing the book. Whether there are any occult or mystic influences mixed up with the reasons mentioned can be better told after it is finished than now in its preliminary pages. I am inclined to indorse most heartily, from close observation of the matter, the affirmation of the quaint Thoreau, sometimes called the Walden hermit: "We should consider that the flow of thought is more like a tidal wave than a prone river, and is the result of a celestial influence, not of any declivity in its channel."

" Where are now the fabled beings that peopled space,
That had their haunts in dale or piny mountain,
Or forest by slow stream, or pebbly spring,
Or chasm, or wat'ry depths? All these have vanished;
They live no longer in the faith of reason !
But still the heart doth need a language; still
Doth the old instinct bring back the old names,
And to yon starry world they now are gone;
Spirits, or gods, that used to share this earth
With man as with their friends.
Oh, never more will I blame his faith,
In the might of stars and angels
This visible nature and this common world
Is all too narrow."—*Coleridge.*

25

II.

A substitute for faith. — The Bible a sealed book without it. — With it, a rational one.

Modern Spiritualism is not so much a matter of argument as it is a matter of experience; still some may like to know a little of the experience that has made me (who am something of a worldly man, or one who has touched the world rather broadly) one of its adherents. Its truth, or foundation in fact, came to me in such a perfectly satisfactory manner over a quarter of a century ago that it established itself in my mind, and has been my religion ever since. No one can foretell with certainty how the future may find him, but I think it one of the certain things in my future career that I will not backslide or fall from its grace; that it has come to me to stay, and, as it is my religion now, so will it continue to be.

It certainly ought to be true. If death ended all, and there was no future conscious life to departed human beings, that when a man died that was the end of him, certainly to most people this life would be a failure. A continuation of a man's career

27

beyond the grave, from a human standpoint, is demanded on the score of justice. The Christian, or civilized world, sees that everywhere, and rests its hope on Divine revelation, or God's word, for assurance. If the Bible were God's word, that would be an assurance. That holy and very valuable old book has, however, a very human flavor. God may speak in it, or through it, but certainly not in any real or literal manner. He speaks through it only as the Great First Cause speaks in and through everything in the world around us, and in the heavens above us. Men in old times, as now, may have been inspired, and uttered or written wise thoughts even beyond their own normal powers, many of them worthy of high sources, but certainly no one in this age will consider the Bible as God's word literally in any sense, even admitting it to be the most valuable book extant. My experience in spiritual manifestations has enhanced its value to me, because I see permeating that book, from Genesis to Revelations, evidences of an intelligent spiritual environment, interested in and influencing mankind, and that, also, is the teaching of modern Spiritualism today. Expressed by a modern poet thus: —

"The spirit world, around this world of sense,
    Rests like an atmosphere, and everywhere
Wafts through these earthly mists and vapors dense,
    A vital breath of more ethereal air."

In an age when this world was the center of the universe, and the sun a ball of molten iron about the

size of the territory of Greece, these influences, or
" strange visitants " from this environment, were mis-
understood, intentionally or otherwise. In one case,
it will be remembered, a correction was made by the
angel, or divine messenger, or departed spirit, by his
saying to the saintly apostle : " I am one of thy brethren of the prophets." At last we are learning to take
the spirit of that book and not its letter, but that does
not make the basis of a future life any better, or any
more certain, for the definition of the spirit of it will
vary in differently constituted minds; in the last
analysis it becomes nothing but human testimony,
and of no authority. In fact, the Bible is a sealed
book without modern Spiritualism. Interpreted by
it, there is proof that man survives death, but that
makes one a Spiritualist. Outside of modern Spiritualism there is no proof that the man survives the
death of his body. Helped by this later light, many
things in the Bible, and outside of it, become pointers, or proofs, of man's survival, but that aid is the
property of and belongs to modern Spiritualism.

To make a future conscious life certain one must
return from the dead, or a message must come
from one who has ended his mortal career, and it
must be unmistakable.

> "Ah! blow me the scent of one lily, to tell
>   That it grew outside of the world at most;
> Ah! show me a plume to touch, or a shell
>   That whispers of some unearthly coast,"

is what the hungry human heart says, and has a right
to say, and that is what modern Spiritualism claims

to do, and what it certainly has done to me. It is the object of these chapters, which I have called "Shadows," to try to establish that claim. I hardly expect to do it, for the reason already stated, that the subject is more a matter of experience than of argument; but we will do the best we can, and we will certainly be truthful,

> "and give to our airy 'something'
> A local habitation and a name."

Intuitive souls all over the world, and all through the ages, have felt their immortality, and the earth itself is ominous with the idea. The poet interviews it with his soul, and utters his thought in verse, speaking wiser than he knows, and thus often breathing the spirit of man's post-mortem life; hungry humanity reads the sentiment, and wishes it was real, as well as poetic. One message from the world of spirits, one soul returning after having passed through death, would change poetry into truth, and bring the heart's intuitions into the domain of the positive. Until that message comes, or that "departed" one returns, the woman of Endor may raise Samuel, Moses and Elias be transfigured before Peter, James and John and the Revelator bow before the angel, and Hamlet may see the ghost of the royal Dane armed, *cap-a-pie*, and Longfellow may tell in his pensive, almost truthful, way that

> "Through the open doors
> The harmless phantoms on their errands glide
> With feet that make no noise upon the floors.

> We meet them at the door-way, on the stair,
>   Along the passages they come and go,
> Impalpable impressions on the air,
>   A sense of something moving to and fro; "

and nervous women may see sainted shadows pass
the open doors of darkened rooms that even prove
sometimes to be premonitions; but they are all
"such stuff as dreams are made of," whether records
of revelation or drafts of imagination bodying forth
the forms of things unseen for the poet's pen to
mold into shape; they are punctured bubbles, van-
ishing in the light of reason and common sense, and
are at best but what the following agnostic lines express : —

> " The hollow sea-shell, which for years hath stood
>   On dusty shelves, when held against the ear
>   Proclaims its stormy parent, and we hear
> The faint, far murmur of the distant flood.
> We hear the sea. The sea? It is the blood
>   In our own veins, impetuous and near,
>   And pulses keeping pace with hope and fear.
> So in my heart I hear, as in a shell,
>   Distinct, distinct, though faint and far it be.
> Thou fool! this echo is a cheat as well,
>   The hum of earthly instincts; and we crave
>   A world unreal as the shell-heard sea."

If modern Spiritualism has any basis, any *raison
d'être* in its claim, that there are messages from the
loved and lost, that the spirit world can, and does,
more or less intelligently, communicate with the inhabitants of earth; and if this is true, the ideal world becomes more or less a real one, many a fascinating fable
becomes a reality, and it puts a torch behind the cur-

tain in the picture of human life, making it a transparency of light and warmth, as well as beauty. And we can feel it to be really so when the poet says: —

> " That ever near us, though unseen,
> The dear immortals tread;
> For all the boundless universe
> Is life,— there are no dead."

"Can it be true, this wondrous story old,
    Of fair green pastures where the waters flow
    In sweetest music over golden sands,
    Where we shall meet again the lost of earth?
            Can such a country be
    As this of which our hopeful spirits dream,
    For which we yearn, and hope, and trust, and pray
    Such prayers to Him, the Being Infinite?
    Oh! can it be that we shall grasp again
    The cold white hands which here we fold to rest
    Upon the breast, thrilling with life anew?
    And feel again upon our lips and brow
    The kisses of the lips that have grown cold
    While kissing us? And is the grave
    Only a narrow gate, through which we pass
    To peace and rest and calm?"—*Anonymous.*

III.

THE GATES AJAR.

*Explaining why the writer is a Spiritualist, and why
obliged to be one.*

When death entered my family, we had three
young children; the oldest was a girl. She was six
years old when death took her. I had a religious
experience in my early life, was a church-member for
a decade. At the period of this grief I was, and had
been for many years, a materialist. When this little
girl's light went out, leaving us in the dark, I felt
that that was the end of her. The mother took the
loss naturally harder than I did. I was, and am, of
a philosophical turn of mind, and considered this the
fate and the end of all; but it had come early to this
bright flower in the garden of our home. As there
was no help for it, it must be submitted to. This
was our grief. The mother, it may have been providential, and, from later experiences, I think it was,
came accidentally in contact with some of those who
were interested in the new light of modern Spiritualism, and seeing a medium was suggested to her. As
the drowning man catches at a straw, she caught at

this. Afterwards, when hearing her report of what she had heard and seen in her contact with the subject from time to time, it seemed silly business, and made no impression upon me; but I saw no harm in it, as it occupied her mind, and gave her something to think of. My wife was not reconciled to the loss of our child, and looking into this matter might be a harmless benefit to her, but otherwise I saw no sense in it, and certainly none in the phenomena, as she related to me from time to time what took place. I could not see anything sensible in supposing spirits made raps, or of the tipping of tables, or any perception of clairvoyant images of little girls that nobody could see but the medium, or woman who called herself a seeress. I think it grieved my wife that I did not interest myself more, and it seemed to partake a little of cold-heartedness on my part. She was wrong there, for I was all feeling, but felt, as the majority feel today, that the subject was beneath the notice or attention of sensible people. My wife having confidence in me and my acuteness, thought I could and ought to settle this matter as either something or nothing. I felt, as a matter of course, that it was a delusion. I hated to stoop to conquer it, and I saw it was occupying her mind, and it was, at best, an innocent amusement. This interest continued many weeks, even a month or two, and was my wife's principal thought, and I hated to disabuse her of it, and yet, from what I heard or read in the papers, I began to have fears that it possibly might be an injury, and I had begun to think to myself how I could adroitly puncture it so that she could see it herself to be a delusion without any overt act of mine, for I felt that I would be belittling myself to meddle with it as I would to go to a Gypsy to get my fortune told.

Early one afternoon, just as she was going out for a walk or a call, she met her sister on the steps just coming to see her. After exchanging a few words, my wife said to her sister that she was going to see a medium, and asked her if she did not want to go to. The sister had never been at or heard of such sittings, rather liked the idea, and they went together, it seems to me it was to a Mrs. Leeds, of whom my wife had incidentally heard. On reaching the house in Carver Street, they found Mrs. Leeds was absent on a visit to Judge Edmonds, in New York. They were, of course, disappointed, and, turning to go away, they asked the girl who had waited on the door if she knew any good medium, and she gave them the address of Mrs. Hayden, of Hayward Place, and the ladies went directly there.

I am being very minute in relating this occurrence, as it turned out to be the "Dawning Light" to me, and would to anyone under the same circumstances, as it covers the whole ground claimed by modern Spiritualism, and every solution for it conceivable, and nothing but an admittance of the truth of it, as founded in fact, can explain this one experience.

I never conversed with an intelligent person who did not admit that it compelled a belief, if the facts were as I have stated them. Hence my being so particular in this narrative which I offer, as I do in fact the whole of this book as well as this chapter, as the exact truth.

I was left at home, as these ladies departed, I knowing nothing of their intentions. I did not know where they were going, or that they had started on a spiritual expedition. What I have said in the foregoing lines I learned afterwards, and the following cogitative and circumstantial statement will explain it: —

I was in my library up stairs, and alone. I had some writing to do, but the subject of spiritual manifestations was for the moment occupying my mind, and in their connection with my wife who had just gone out, as I have described, and I began to cogitate. I said to myself, ought I not to look into this matter, and why is it necessary to go to a stranger to get a message from any of my departed friends? That has, thought I, an unreasonable look to begin with. I had forgotten, or it did not occur to me, that King Saul, when in grief and sore distressed, had to go in that way to the woman of Endor before he could connect himself with or get a message from his departed friend Samuel. In beginning this cogitation, it rather appeared to me that if my little daughter was alive, though invisible, or any spirit of my loved and lost relatives or friends had any message for me, here and now was the time and place for the manifestations. Here in this room is the old table, and on it the old Bible, printed in 1751, that old familiar faces of my youth sat at and turned the leaves of the book, and show and explain the pic-

tures in it, and I began to grow sentimental with the
pleasures of memory. I seemed to grow hospitable
to the idea, or rather to the images of these old faces
that were as vivid, in my mind, as the old book was
that had outlasted them to my senses. I believed
everything was subject to law, and that it was possible that the room was then full of spirits, though my
intellect was infidel to the idea; still in my heart there
arose a sacred voice which said it was a possible thing.
Perhaps there is something wanting which I have
not got, thought I, which, if I had, or was in the
right condition, these old familiar faces, or some of
them, might issue out of the silent air, or in some
way manifest or reach me. Some remembrances of
family love, that need not be mentioned now, but
may be before this book is ended, had some effect
upon me, and I began to dwell on it in my imagination,— build castles in the air, as some call it,— I did
alone what I would have been ashamed to have done
in any company. I said to the circumambient, vacant
air vocally, if there are any beings present who
can hear me (thinking then of my child, Hattie,
and my sister), I wish you would be present when
my wife attends any of these sittings, and will you
send me a message? and remembering I had had
messages now and then,— love-sending, or remembrances which had no convincing character to them,
and what anyone could say, and not be out of the
way; so I said, send me this message,— which I then
repeated. I will not repeat here the message I asked
for; it was characteristic of me, and was religiously

asked for, but it might be construed humorously, and in the connection seem frivolous, for though I am constitutionally light-hearted and cheerful, I have a very pensive undertone, and on this subject, whatever may be my manner, I am at heart always serious.

It occurred to me, also, that spirits might see and not hear, and, having a pen before me, I wrote the message as well as spoke it, and folded up the paper on which it was written, and put it into my desk, where no one could see or get it. I certainly did not expect any response. I did not ask for it with any faith. I do not know as if I ever would have thought of it again, except that the subject, in its connection with my wife, was often in my mind, and this trifling circumstance would, therefore, not have been forgotten. I however had the feeling that I would give all I had in the world if there had been any foundation of truth in this matter, which, however, did not seem to me at all probable or possible.

I did not know, as I have already said, where my wife had gone. What I had said, thought, and done alone in my library was known only to myself. Late in the afternoon I went out, and on my return at tea-time, the first thing my wife said to me was: "There is a message for you from Hattie," handing me a small, rolled-up strip of paper, she looking at me, all alive with expectation, for she knew, under any circumstances, the message would please me, as a definitely characteristic one, of or for me. I unrolled, read it, and found a long string of letters not divided into words, but it was the message exactly, when divided off into words, that I had asked for a few hours before.

Now, suppose I am telling the exact truth, setting nothing down for effect or for argument, and I assure the reader such is the fact exactly as I have stated it, — what else can it be but the message from a spirit? It purported to come from Hattie; but she could not write. She was a little girl only a few months over six years old; but that is a matter of minor importance. Did it come from the other world? That settled, settles the whole matter; and how could it have been anything else? This matter being so important, some reflections and deductions will not be superfluous.

There was certainly no mind-reading (mind-reading seems to be the *bête noir* of the skeptic in this department of thought), for I concocted the message alone, and I was not present at this Endoric interview. No one knew but myself what I had done but the "circumambient air," or the invisible dwellers in it, and of course around me. My wife and her sister knew nothing of it, and if the medium had been a fraud and had made the raps herself, she must have had a royal road of information to have got cognizance of my act or wishes. I did not know there was such a woman in the world. It was the first time my wife had ever been at her house, and did not know she was going there when she left home. The reader will remember she got the address from a domestic at a house where she had never been, and was unknown, and Hayward Place was over a mile off

from where I lived, and had had this private colloquy
with what I now consider my spiritual surrounding,
or environment.

So, look at the matter in any light one chooses, if
the writer's head is level, and is telling the truth,
there certainly was a message from "over the river."
If anyone doubts me, thinks I am a special pleader
for the cause, and am overstating, when I assure him
I am exact and truthful, then this book of "shadows" is not for him, and he may as well skip me and
pass on to something that, to him, will be more interesting or instructive.

As I have said, I feel like being very particular,
and, perhaps, long-drawn out in this statement more
than I intend to be in the chapters that follow, for
this one experience is, in the writer's mind, a clincher,
so to speak, and settles the whole question in his
mind affirmatively. I will now close it with a brief
account of the sitting itself.

These ladies, when they reached the medium's
house in Hayward Place, found there the lady, and
stated what they had come for, and were invited to
sit down at the table used for the purpose of spirit
communications, the medium sitting at it also. The
sister held the pencil,—she had been requested to
by my wife before entering, to see if it made any
difference. Raps were at once heard, the spirits answering yes and no to questions. Soon the alphabet
was used, and as the letter wanted was reached a rap
was heard, and thus some singular but very true
messages were given intelligently in this way, but

they need not be recorded here. After a little while the letters of a message read: *"Hattie is here:"* My wife said: "I am glad you have come; have you anything to say to your father?"—and three raps indicated "Yes." The alphabet was then used, and the letters noted down as the raps signified the right one; and, when finished, it was a string of letters, as I have said, not divided into words, but which were easily read, particularly by my wife, who saw that it was somewhat characteristic, and knew it would please me, and perhaps be a test. She did not know until she had got home and given it to me, and I had told her the facts, that I had asked the spirits to send the message, and the string of letters written down in that way,—the letter wanted being rapped at when it was reached,—and in their wholeness was the message I had asked for in the manner stated.

As a finish to this chapter, let me close with a suggestive verse or two that I find in my scrap-book, and then the reader can do his own thinking:—

"But, hark! I hear a gentle rap,
  Most strange to human ears!
May it not be some message sent
  From those bright-shining spheres?

The questions put, the answers come
  As plain as A, B, C,
Which tell me that departed friends
  Are coming back to me.

No voice I hear, no form behold,
  And yet I feel impressed
The loving message surely comes
  From loved ones gone to rest."

"I have reason to think it no delusion —
    And therefore fancy that my child is near,
And so I feel amid this world's confusion
    The influence of her serener sphere.
I doubt if she is in the church-yard sleeping,
    And have at last become aware
That she eluded us while we were weeping,
    And that my child was never buried there."

—*Anonymous.*

45

IV.

*Its permanent entrance into the writer's mental life.
—Details of the interview.*

When I received and read the message that in this mysterious way (as I have stated in the preceding chapter) had come from the spirit of my little daughter that I had seen laid in the tomb a few months before, it surprised me very much, it was certainly so unexpected. I knew I held the secret as surely as Junius did of his "letters," but here was my message, word for word. My request must have been heard by the invisible intelligences in that room where I was sitting and cogitating alone, who must have known the location of my wife, where she had gone, for I did not, so they could not have got it from my mind, and who there, at that sitting, answered me. Does it not look as if, all unseen by me, I was open and visible to some of my departed friends in the spirit world? as if they, knowing my wishes, had said: "Let us go to that seance where his wife, our sister or mother had gone, and see if we cannot prove to him that he is encompassed round about with intelligences;" or, as expressed in the words of Mrs. Harriet Beecher Stowe : —

> " It is a beautiful belief,
>   That ever round our head
>   Are hovering with viewless wings
>   The spirits of the dead."

I do not know why I should be so much favored when so many better and wiser men, as hungry for the truth as I am, have been slighted. And then I have asked a great many times since for a similar manifestation for just such a purpose, but the "vacant air" has been deaf. Angels' visits of the kind most wanted are, indeed, few and far between; perhaps I have had my share of attention. Here is the fact once anyway; perhaps that was a compensation for other deficiencies, but that is not the point to be treated now.

I have had a quarter of a century of experience in spiritual matters. A large percentage of it is of no account. The identification of a spirit is a very difficult thing to do. I have had hundreds of proofs of spirits communicating with me to one of identification. I think I could discount seventy-five per cent of my experiences in this line of thought, and the substance of the whole might be included in the remaining one-quarter, or twenty-five per cent. Some may think I have wasted a great deal of time in washing, so to speak, in this lean gulch, and the amount of gold gathered has been small for the time and labor spent; but what I have got is what I want, and what the world wants today, more than anything else, and is not to be found outside of "these diggings." Where in the whole world of thought can one find such a nugget of value as the message and the circumstances of which I have spoken in the last chapter. If it had never been duplicated (and it never has exactly, and seldom anything near it) it would, as I have said, have settled the matter in my own mind. I feel thankful for succeeding so well the first time, for it has encouraged me in years of lean perseverance, so that I never was discouraged, even if not always satisfied; but all along the years of my experience in these matters have I found (though sometimes it may have been at long intervals) nuggets of value that are evidences of the truth for which I was seeking.

When this message from Hattie came to me, I went at once to see this modern woman of Endor, to see if she could raise any of my Samuels. I went into her parlor a stranger both to her and to the subject. She was sitting on a sofa in her modestly-furnished room; near the center of it was a round, mahogany table. I hardly knew what to say, or what to do. It was new business to me. The lady helped me by saying: "Do you want to talk with the spirits?" I said: "Most certainly." She remarked, in a courteous manner, that there were a great many here, or that I had brought a great many with me. She said: "Take a seat at the table," pointing to the one I had noticed, which was about three feet from her. I did so, moving it a little so as to detect any deceptive mechanism, for I was of a suspicious nature, at least in a matter of this kind. She, noticing it, said: "That's right; put the table anywhere you please." Her manners pleased me; she seemed honest; I was satisfied, and sat down to it, my hands resting on it.

It seems now that I ought to narrate, in tolerable detail, the circumstances of this my first interview with the spirits of the other world; but it seems to me also that they ought to have been on some elevated matters, and not at all common-place, and which seem almost, when dealing with the dead, or rather "departed." trifling. The query arises in my mind now whether I had not better compose a presentation analogously true, but one more in conformity with one's expectation from such a supposed source, the heavenly world. I think this would be the way usually such a matter would be given to the public, and not draw out of obscurity the domestic social life and names of quiet, unknown people. Yet, if a person that I respected, and was worth listening to, was talking to me, I would want the simple facts, and when given, as they have been colloqually often by me, they have always been impressively interesting, and as I am with sincerity, and also simplicity, now talking with the reader, I think the literal statement, with this apology, will be the best one. My hesitancy is owing in a measure from feeling, or did feel at the time, and as others do at that stage of their belief, that the spirit world was a sanctified and holy place, and that one must feel serious or religious when dealing with it. There was nothing serious or religious in the pabulum that then came to me from that world of light. Yet there was a charming and complicated truthfulness in it, and that, after all, is the main thing. Some one has said the laws of crystalization, manifested in the freezing of ditch water, are as interesting a study as they are in the crystalization of the diamond; so I trust in this trifle that I propose to relate,.as the illustrative point,—the underlying laws,—will make my simple water diamondish in character.

I came to this medium's house under the assumed name of Johnson, and, hearing the raps, was told they were the spirits, and that I could ask them any questions. I began by asking the invisible if they knew me, and the reply being "Yes," I said: "What is my name?" and the answer was, "John Wetherbee." I was both surprised and interested, for, as I have said, I was entirely unknown to the medium, and though she sat very near the table, I could see she did not touch it, and if she had, under all the circumstances, it would have made no difference. I then asked: "Will you tell me who you are?" And the raps spelled the name of "Susan Gibson."

I was expecting it would have been Adeline, Hattie, or some other near spirit, and I did not know any Susan Gibson; and hoping to bring her to mind, among other questions, I said: "Where did you die?" The reply was: "Providence." That fact did not help any, but was interesting, as I had relatives in that city, and had visited it a great deal. I then asked: "When did you die?" And the reply was: "About nine years ago." This was interesting, for my sister was living there; had been married a year or more before that time. My unmarried sister was a guest of hers much of the time, and for the year or two prior to the nine years mentioned by the spirit, I was there near half of my time, and so I concluded that Susan Gibson might have been some person that I had met there that I had forgotten, though it seems she had not forgotten me. I then asked the spirit: "Do you know my sister?" The reply was: "Yes." "What is her name?" And the letters, in reply, rapped out were, E L I. Noticing them thus, I thought to myself she is mistaken; it is going to be Eliza or Elizabeth, and I have no sister by that name. I said nothing, and the next letter was an O, then a T, and the rapping stopped. At first, I did not recognize it, but as quickly as I saw it read, Eliot, then I saw it was my sister's name, Elliott. The spirit had spelled the name in the usual way, but our Elliotts spelled it with two l's and two t's, and in the diminished form I at first did not recognize it. It was far better in the way manifested, for it showed the spirit was not getting it from my mind. I then saw that that was the name of my living sister; but I wanted the name of my dead one, or who was now a spirit, and the reply was: "Adeline," which was correct.

Speaking of this to my sister in Providence, I found her no better off than I was; she could remember no Susan Gibson among her acquaintances, but in the early part of her married life — say ten or eleven years before this interview — she had a domestic living with her by the name of Susan ; it might have been Susan Gibson, but she did not know whether it was or not. As the communication was so correct, even free from any mind-reading, it seems to me reasonable to suppose it was the Susan that was the domestic. Imagine the situation, and see how natural it is, on that basis. She was the family-servant of Mrs. Elliott, my sister visiting her, whose name was Adeline, and I was often there. I asked her, as a spirit, for my sister's name. I was thinking of Adeline, who was a spirit, but the spirit of the domestic said "Eliot," speaking of her mistress by the name she was known, and then of Adeline, as she would have been known in that household. In the long, tedious way of getting messages, with the aid of an alphabet, one cannot use superfluous words any more than one does in a telegram. If Susan had been giving those messages in her living state, or a free translation of them into a polite vernacular, they would read : "Your living sister's name is Mrs. Eliot, and the sister who is now a spirit her name is Miss Adeline." We must understand the superfluous appellations *Mrs.* and *Miss* are understood, and not necessarily expressed in spiritual as well as in telegraphic messages.

" It is the hour of prayer. All day the din of active life over-whelms, and the latent soul speaks not. Thankful are we for the return of evening, bringing us back to serious thought, when hearts speak and voices oft are silent,—vain wanderings o'er a sea of thoughts we cannot fathom. It is the hour when children talk with angels. It is the hour we feel our immortal-ity. It is the hour when old familiar faces look at us from the dark corners of the room. Old portraits on the wall attract expression, and the recognitions make us feel their living pres-ence. Can the witching hour of twilight make vivid the shadows of loved faces who dwell beyond the vale,—whose silent voices ignite thought, whose footsteps leave no track behind?"

— Shadows.

V.

LIFE'S AFTERNOON.

The "Dawning Light" seems to be a boon or consola-
tion to advancing years.—An extension-claim.

> "The day is past and gone,
> The evening shades appear;
> Oh, may we all remember well
> The night of death draws near."

There is a religious association that comes up in
the mind with this oft-repeated and oft-sung hymn
to which no reference is now intended. Take it as
it reads,—not its associations, or what in a pious direction it may suggest,—how differently the thought
strikes the mind of a youth of twenty from what it
does the adult, or mature one of sixty!

The grim messenger, as death is sometimes called,
is near youth, of course; but when one is thus early
called, it seems somewhat out of order,—a mistake
somewhere, a payment anticipated, one made before
it was due. When the noon of a man's life is past,
or if it is four o'clock or five or six in the afternoon
of his life, the sun nearing his western horizon,—the
"Night of Death,"—then is a vivid point; it seems

57

near or nearer then, mathematically, no matter how much of time there still may be left for him.

It is wisely provided that youth and young manhood should be hopeful, and even thoughtless, and death but lightly considered. With sixty years of probable life before a man, or only six, the future prospect differs. When one reads a thoughtful verse like this, which is so suggestive and truthful also,—

"The end of life comes nearer,
　　Every year;
The friends left become dearer,
　　Every year;
And the goal of all that 's mortal,
Opens wider still its portal
To the land of the immortal,
　　Every year,"

it will strike the mind of a man who, on the principle of life assurance or of annuities, has fifty years before him very differently from one whose chances are but for five, or ten, on the statistical ground. It is well that it is so, for the youth has the world's affairs on his hands, the old man more naturally begins to set his house in order.

Modern Spiritualism then seems to come as a boon or a comfort to old people. It is a beautiful and inspiring thought to the young also, especially if the pale angel is beckoning to one. These "anticipated payments" are very common. There comes a time also when the end of life is falling due, in the natural order of things. Three-score-and-ten is an indefinite point in one's lifetime, though definitely expressed, but is reached by all, like a promissory note falling due. It is only a question of time.

How cheering, then, the thought that the little span of life that a man sees before him when he reaches nearer and nearer this indefinite but certain point is extended into a perpetuity — a continuous life — under new conditions. That is what modern Spiritualism teaches, and, if based on truth, what an acquisition it is!

In the light of some facts, which will appear in the course of these chapters, how can it be anything else but what it claims to be? This extension of life is not exactly an ethereal one, but one as real to the senses as this one is that we are now living. It seems to be a very human life, if not a mortal one. Our aims and tastes, and sometimes our misfortunes here, are continued there on, perhaps, a higher plane or outlook, the misfortunes here being the beginnings of what may be successes there, and possibly viewing them retrospectively may be the most lustrous ones of our human experience. To be sure there is no ticketing our baggage through the gates of death to the summer land. All our wealth is left on this side of the grave,— useful here, of no account there.

What empty bags some of our rich people — even millionaires — must be when discretely separated from their possessions! How important for. such, and all, to keep a sinking-fund of enduring possessions as this life's years glide by that will be income-producing (using our vernacular) when this life's fitful fever is over! It may not be out of place to quote a communication that this latter remark suggests that came to me once through the medium Mary Hardy, she being unconscious,—in a trance.

This was from an aged, well-known citizen, an intimate friend of mine, who had departed from this life some years before. Besides the communication, I could give some circumstances that insure its genuineness, but I must refrain from doing so here for the sake of brevity. Please take my word for it, and read the characteristic message. I do not quote it as evidence of spirit existence, though I receive it as such myself, from the circumstances referred to attending it, but which would not be of any interest to the general reader. The communication itself will be illustrative of the idea above suggested, of keeping a "sinking fund" that will be, in a spiritual sense, income-producing "in the sweet by-and-bye."

"Summer-Land securities, like the securities current on 'change, do not come by the asking, or by inheritance, they all have to be earned. A man may be poor in one and may be rich in the other. The former boil no pots, and in the affairs of life, or the settlement of estates, are not counted as assets. Successful business men often make a poor showing when they close in on the mortal and open out into the immortal state.

"There is but one way by which the gilt-edged securities of earth can be converted into the gilt-edged of the Summer Land, and that is by unselfish uses. Both kinds are in your market now; the enduring find comparatively but few takers, the passing are in active demand. If I had known ten years ago what I know now, I would have left less money to my heirs, but I would have been more affluent now. I did, you know, an unselfish act of considerable magnitude, and worried some about it. I was glad before I died that I did it, and I am gladder still now. It has proved to be the best investment I have now in this Summer Land, and it makes me quite comfortable."

The principal feature in the teachings of modern Spiritualism is that the grave is not merely a hole in the ground, or blind alley, but, figuratively speaking, is a thoroughfare opening out into eternal light. Our night of death comes, but our life is not ended. Our day may have ended and its work done, but we awake and find it the morning of a new day.

I do not know how it is with other people, but to me this extension of our life beyond the valley and the shadow of death, and free from its anxieties and troubles, and yet retaining our identities, or conscious *ego*,— our personality,— with a busy and progressive future, is a joyous vision, an inheritance of priceless value.

It changes the whole aspect of human life, and certainly adds sunshine to the remainder of this, which cannot now be, to this writer, but a decade or two at most. Though, as I have said, this sometimes called the "Dawning Light" is the bright gift to old age, and it is the bright gift to all who are open-eyed to it, and to all, anyway, at last, for "old age" is the possibility of all; so, in time, these suggestions will be in order for all those who have been lucky enough to have been undrafted from their life in the former, until (using a mercantile phrase) they have become due.

I have a friend, whose ancestors lived in this old Bay State; but, in the long ago, his parents emigrated to the far west, and grew up with it in what is now the State of Iowa. While writing this chapter, I have received a letter from him. Its contents seem almost a contribution to, or corroboration of, what I have been saying. His communication embraced the celebration of the ninety-first anniversary of the birth-day of his mother,— in good health, for her years, and mind unclouded.

I have always been pleased with the tender and rational tones of his poetic effusions on previous similar and other festive occasions which he has generally sent to me, as he has this one. At this time were gathered children, grandchildren, and relatives and friends; and he among them gave and read a poetic tribute, which the old lady and all enjoyed for its beauty and fitness. He, like this writer, is getting to be somewhat venerable, but our souls are young, as, on my theory, all Spiritualists' *souls* ought to be; and the fact of being believers in our hopeful philosophy takes these tributes out of mere poetry and sentiment, and gives the luster of reality, that no one who does not only feel, but knows, that this life is but the vestibule of the one that follows, can realize these mortal sunsets so radient with blue, green, and gold, bespeaking a pleasant day on the "tomorrow of death," as a true Spiritualist can.

Feeling now in this special case more than it may

be prudent to say in a book, I will print his verses for the sake of their preservation, and as a reminder to this writer and others of much that is suggested but not expressed here.

ANNIVERSARIUS.*

"October, seventeen ninety-three,
Shall ever to us children be
A month and year of jubilee;
For then was born to life and light
The being of our heart's delight,
Who modestly through life's long flight,
Hath honor's shield kept clean and bright,—
      Our mother.

Who in our country's early dawn
Hath listened, rapt, to tales and song
Of Washington and Jefferson,
Amidst New England's Christian spires,
Of lofty deeds through battle's fires
That Freedom won for glorious sires,—
      Our mother.

Who in young womanhood's first grace
Hath joined her brothers in the race
Through forests dark new paths to trace;
And plant new States on fields afar,
Where brightly shone that 'Western Star'
Which hostile foes should ne'er debar,—
      Our mother.

Full many a task is bravely done,
Full many a trial nobly won,
Through her ripe years of ninety-one.
May peace and honor crown her days;
Let trust in God her courage raise,
While all her children join to praise,—
      Our mother."

* C. A. K.—Keokuk, October 28, 1884.

In the course of this chapter, which seems to have
been inspired by what might be called the approach
of evening, one may have noticed a thoughtfully-
expressed verse from an "Old Man's Story." I do
not know who was the author, but think I will use
the rest of it, it expresses so well what I want to say,
and better than I can say it in prose briefly. I do
not think the author will object to my thus drafting
it from my scrap-book, with the setting I have thus
given to his words, which are as follows: —

"To the past go more dead faces
　　　Every year,
As the loved leave vacant places
　　　Every year.
Everywhere the sad eyes meet us,
In the evening dusk they greet us,
And to come to them entreat us
　　　Every year.

You are growing old, they tell us,
　　　Every year;
You are more alone, they tell us,
　　　Every year;
You can win no more affection,
You have only recollection,
Deeper sorrow and dejection,
　　　Every year.

Yes, the shores of life are shifting
　　　Every year,
And we are all seaward drifting
　　　Every year;
Old places changing, fret us,
The living now forget us,
There are fewer to regret us
　　　Every year.

But the truer life draws nigher
          Every year,
And its morning star climbs higher
          Every year;
Earth's hold on us grows slighter,
And the heavy burdens lighter,
And the dawn of the immortal brighter,
          Every year."

" All who appreciate the influence of high ideals, and an exalted faith in immortality on individual and national destiny, must admit that the transit of a pencil, proved beyond a doubt to be guided by unseen force and intelligence, is a phenomenon of infinitely more value and concern to the world today than the whole science of astronomy."—*Epes Sargent.*

VI.

INDEPENDENT SLATE—WRITING.

*An elaborate description of an experience under the
most rigid conditions.*

One of the most interesting and satisfying phases
of the spiritual phenomena is independent slate-writing. It interested the late Epes Sargent more than any
other phase, and so it does me; but I include writing or written messages made otherwise when I know
them to be genuine, that is, from a super-mundane
source. I think, however, there are many other
phases of the phenomena equally interesting and
important. There is something, nevertheless, that is
very convincing in this slate-writing phase, and I
have had much interesting experience in it.

No one is more aware than I am of its liability to
be fraudulent, but no amount of fraud lessens the
value of a genuine manifestation. Liability of being
cheated should lead us to be open-eyed so as to be
sure of our facts. I am happy to say that I am sure;
and if there are any "bottom facts" in anything,
the facts that I offer under this head, as well as the
facts offered in the other chapters of this book, can
be depended upon as "bottom" ones.

It would require a book by itself to relate all my experiences in this line that are unmistakable, but that is not now the object. I will relate one experience, and do it somewhat elaborately, some of the outcome of it being rather important, because it extended some beyond my personal experience afterwards, even into the public life of Rev. Joseph Cook, and local history.

I was not particularly attracted to Charles E. Watkins, but that, of course, is a matter of taste. I sometimes think Ralph Waldo Emerson must have had the mediumistic class in his mind when he said: "There is a crack in everything that God has made, but the light of heaven shines through the crevice." But this class, so prominent in modern Spiritualism, knows that I appreciate it, and that I do not make this remark as any reflection, only from my experience. I am glad I am not a medium, and I dare say they are glad that they are not this writer. But what would we do without them?

I said I was not much attracted to Watkins, but from my experience with him under crucial test conditions, I think I had been prejudiced, so I say this to do him justice. Meeting him one day in the *Banner of Light* bookstore, he asked me, rather patronizingly, why I had not been to see him or his manifestations, and said he would like to have me do so, if I was willing. I replied that I had not much leisure time for such things, except for my own benefit, and then I wanted to have everything my own way. "You can have everything your own way," said he, "if you will come." I said: "If you mean exactly that, Mr. Watkins, I will come and have a sitting with you." He replied that he did mean exactly that, and I fixed the next day in the afternoon, at three o'clock, as the time that I would call upon him. I hope the reader will notice very particularly, and in detail, my method, and as I intend to be very exact, and the result being very important, my statement will be worth listening to.

The next day, on my way to his residence, I stopped at a hardware store on Washington Street, and bought two new slates. In size they were about twelve inches by eight, with the usual wooden frames. As the storekeeper had no double slates, I got him to bore a hole through them both on their sides, through which I run a strong twine, and tied them together, making them practically a double slate, putting between them a small bit of slate pencil before tying them thus together. I then, in that form, knowing they were new and clean, put them into my bag, which, as usual, I was carrying, and continued my way to Mr. Watkins's residence. I found him at home and alone in his parlor.

It was one of the long, warm days of summer, the curtains were up, and the bright afternoon sun was shining into the room, so it was very light, and one could read easily in any part of it. There were sofa and chairs in the room, and in the center was a plain, wooden table, rectangular in shape, about four feet long and two wide. On the table, on one side, were two slates.

I kept my satchel in my hands, and took my seat at the table as he suggested, Mr. Watkins taking his seat at the table, and was my *vis-a-vis*. Being seated, he said: "Wetherbee, now take the slates there" [pointing to those on the table] "to the sink, and see that they are perfectly clean. I do n't want to touch them," said he, "for the better test; the manifestation will be to you, if we get any." "That is very fair," said I, "but I have brought my own slates" [taking them out of my bag], "and I guess I will use them." "That is right," said he; "I am glad you did so."

The slates I took out of the bag just as they were tied together in the store; they had never been out of my hands from the time I had tied them and put them in the bag; then laid them before me flat on the table, and laid my two hands flat on them just as they laid tied together, one then, of course, on the top of the other. The medium, who was sitting, as I have said, opposite to me, in a short time placed his two hands on the top of mine,— mine being unmoved and flat on the slates as I had first put them, and the tied slates one on top of the other flat on the table under my two hands. I hardly think his hands touched the slates; possibly his fingers did slightly; it would make no difference if they had, for the slates nor my hands were not moved from where I first put them.

Nothing occurred for a few minutes, when he said it will probably take longer for the spirits with new unmagnetized slates than it would if I had used his.

I told him I was in no hurry; that there would be a great satisfaction to me if the spirits would write on these new ones of mine, not but what it would be all right for them to use his, but if I afterwards should have occasion to speak of it, it would not carry the same conviction as it would if done on these new ones, and which had never been apart since I tied them together in the store. I must confess I had taken such a rigid course to prevent any fraud or imposition that I hardly expected any writing would be produced. I only hoped without much faith.

In a little while, to my great surprise, I heard a faint but perceptible scratching of, probably, the bit of pencil between the two slates under my hands. The medium's hands were still on mine, and neither his hands nor mine had been moved in the least, and my eyes had not once been off of them. If nothing had been written, it would have been an external sensuous or objective phenomenon, for we both had had auricular evidence that there was some sort of movement without material contact or connection with the operation.

Soon the scratching ended with three pretty distinct taps, seemingly by the pencil inside, and the medium said: "That means they are done." Removing his hands from the top of mine, I then lifted the slates, untied one of the strings, and opened them before me like a double slate, and found on one of the inside faces, in a plain, easy, oblique, running-hand, a message from a well-known departed friend.

It was the name of my father-in-law. The face of

the other slate was untouched and clean. The following is the message that was written by, what it
would seem, invisible hands: —

Summer Land .

"My dear son .

I do thank God that I can give you this test of spirit
power over matter. I trust you will ever strive and search
after truth as you are now   I am truly your father in law

William Beals."

Perhaps it would have been better to have left the
name in blank, but I am aiming to be exact, and so
will be thus outspoken.

I remarked when I read this message, purporting
to come from my venerable friend, that it was quite
remarkable and very satisfactory, for it was written
without mortal contact or mechanical action,— that
is, the bit of pencil was used, it would seem, by an
invisible intelligence, hence must have been done by
a spirit, for no human being in the form did it. The
reader can see that, if I have stated the matter
clearly.

"Do you know the person?" said the medium,
after I had read it. "Oh, yes, perfectly well," said
I, "but it does not sound like him, nor is it his hand-
writing. He wrote rather a bold, perpendicular hand,
—but that is of no consequence. The fact is just
the same, for it is the act of an invisible intelligence,
and no matter who wrote it, I am sure *you* did not,
and no other human being, for we are alone, and if a
spirit wrote it, whether it was my friend or some

alias using his name, it settles the question of a future life."

I do not think the medium knew my connection with the name of that spirit, or any of my social surroundings, and if he had it would not, under such rigid circumstances, have made any difference. He said, in reply to my remark or criticism: "Let us try again."

I closed the slates, and put my hands flat on them as before, and he put his hands on mine. The scratching noise began this time at once, and stopped as before, with three signifying taps, as if with the pencil. On opening them, the other face on which nothing had been written the first time, was the following message. I have them both now, and the slates: —

"My Dear Son. I am going to try & write more like the way I used to, but I may not. Still I want to say tell your wife I still live

William Beals"

It will be noticed that the invisible actor in this matter heard my remark about his hand-writing, for he, she, or it acted on the hint. I do not feel as if this was a message from Mr. Beals. There were more important things to have said if it were he. Still it may have been; but I am sure as I am of anything — in fact, I positively know — that it was not the act of anyone in the form. The proof of identity in the manifestations generally is a far more difficult thing than is the proof of its being a spirit.

I will add, in this connection, that at the bottom of the slate that had the second message written on it was the following message, which was not noticed at first, as it was written very fine, but still very distinctly. It purports to be from my little daughter : —

"Dear father I will now write when you are not expecting me

Your own Hattie "

Not wishing to lose these slates with this experience of perfectly independent slate-writing on them, I tied them up again and put them back into my bag for safe-keeping, and then gave my attention to further manifestations, using the medium's slates, as proposed at first. I will mention but one experiment, which was as follows : —

I took the two slates that were on the table and washed them, though they were clean before, and was going to pass them to him, and was about doing so, holding them both together in my right hand. "No," said he, "I do not want to touch them. Sit down, as before, and hold them together at arm's length as far from me as you can." I did so with my right hand, he sitting *vis-a-vis*, holding my left hand with both of his.

There was, as before, a bit of pencil between the two slates, and, as I held them, they must have been four or five feet from the medium. The writing was at once heard, and there was quite a pressure on the extended slates, so that it was some exertion to hold them out. When the writing had stopped, I laid them open before me, the medium, of course, never having touched them, and there was a letter on each from two of my well-remembered departed friends.

They were written, it would seem, simultaneously, or in the one operation, in entirely different hands and subjects. One, of course, must have been written bottom upwards,— or rather, I should say, the whole operation seems to be a psychical one, or by will-power, rather than by a mechanical one. Here are the two messages, which I copied at the time :—

"How glad I am to come to you Weatherbee and tell you in this way that I am as alive as ever I was and am often with you and am trying to be of service to you
　　Ralph Huntington"

"My son It is very pleasant to prove to you in this way that we can communicate with our friends
　　Wm Beals"

There lacks in these messages the internal evidence of their coming from the parties who have signed them. For instance : my old and intimate friend Ralph Huntington, who also knew my father before me, would never have spelled my name "Weatherbee." Still, we would not criticise, for we do not know the difficulties or disabilities in connection with these occult operations.

On reaching my home after this very satisfactory seance, I saw my friend and neighbor Epes Sargent coming down my street, and I waited at the garden gate for him, and we went into the house together, I having something important to tell him. I showed him the slates that were in my bag, and gave him an account of all the circumstances. He was much pleased, and was very much interested in my account of the experience.

He went in a day or two after that, and had a sitting himself, which, in the end, led to an important circumstance, to be mentioned in another chapter.

Mr. Sargent was entirely unknown to Mr. Watkins. When he called to have a seance, he was not very hospitably received, or, as he would have been, had he announced his name. It was better, however, as it was. Mr. Watkins, it seemed, was not in a good frame of mind, and when this stranger, as it seemed, called to have or see some of his manifestations, the medium was disinclined; said he did not feel very well; did not think he could do anything, and he had better call some other time.

Mr. Sargent said he lived some ways off, and would like very much to have him sit then, as he did not know when he could come again. "Well," says Mr. Watkins, inviting him up stairs, "we will try and see what we can do, but I guess you will be disappointed." Mr. Sargent did not bring any slates, so he sat at the table as I did, and after washing the slates, as he was told to, which then lay on the table, he laid one of them before him, with his two hands upon it. After a little while the bit of pencil which had been placed under it began its perceptible scratching, when suddenly the medium jumped up and said: "Why, you are Epes Sargent;" and the slate was then turned over, at the same time showing a message addressed to Epes Sargent, with his father's name at the end of it.

Now, notice this: it seems that this mysterious work is somehow connected with the mind of the medium, for he had become cognizant that his *vis-a-vis* was Epes Sargent by knowing what the spirit had written on the slate before it had been turned over for the message to be read.

It would seem by this act that the message came into the medium's mind as it was being written on the slate, and before it was turned over to be visible.

This does not alter the super-mundane fact, for it was not in the medium's mind, for he did not know the person before him was Epes Sargent until some exoteric influence had impressed it on his brain, and that seems to have been just when it was being executed on the slate. This was a very interesting point with Mr. Sargent, and more than compensated him for the preliminary inhospitality or brusqueness.

Epes Sargent was one of our distinguished, scholarly Spiritualists. Watkins naturally knew him by reputation, but did not know him personally, having never before met him. Not knowing who his visitor was when he called will account for his indifference, or his state of mind, which so suddenly turned into deference and obsequious civility as soon as he was cognizant from the spirit's message in whose presence he was.

Sargent and I have many times spoken of this circumstance, and as being evidence not only of a royal road for information, but of two distinct personalities,— the personality of the spirit who saw and knew Mr. Sargent, and the personality of Charles E. Watkins, who did not know Mr. Sargent until his invisible assistant had told him who he was by writing his name. True, Watkins knew it intuitively in advance of seeing it, but manifestly not until it had been written by an invisible intelligence.

"Copernicus, reasoning long and patiently about the planet Venus, predicted confidently concerning it before the telescope was invented, that if man ever came to see it more clearly they would discover that it had phases like our moon; and within a century after his death the telescope was invented, and that prediction verified. I am not without hope that we may even here and now obtain some accurate information concerning that 'Other World,' which the instinct of mankind has so long predicted.

Indeed, all that we call science, as well as all we call poetry, is a particle of such information, accurate, as far as it goes, though it be but on the confines of the truth. If we can reason so accurately and with such wonderful confirmation of our reasoning respecting so-called material objects infinitely removed beyond the range of our natural vision, why may not our speculations penetrate as well into the immaterial, starry system of which the former is but the outward and visible type? Surely, we are provided with senses as well fitted to penetrate the spaces of the real, the substantial, the eternal, as those outward are to penetrate the material universe. Veias, Zoroaster, Socrates, Christ, Shakespeare, Swedenburg,— these are some of our astronomers."—*Henry D. Thoreau.*

81

VII.

Thoughts on sensuous phenomena, and illustrations from experience.

The interest felt in the spiritual manifestations is in the fact of their being the work of the spirits of departed human beings. The manifestations in themselves are generally only trifles hardly worthy of attention. My only purpose in writing about them now is wholly owing to what I believe to be their intelligent super-mundane source. There is, however, a difference in them. Some would be interesting simply as physical phenomena, and in this respect those, through the mediumship of Mr. Colchester, were very unique and interesting, and in them I took a great interest and the psychical or will-power in their production, instead of mechanical power on the part of the spirits, or of the medium, if one chooses so to consider it, was a source of light, or, rather, suggested the *rationale* or explanation of many other phases of a more mechanically-performed appearance in their production.

Colchester died a decade or more ago, but many

of the old Spiritualists will remember him well. The thought of him comes up in connection with Epes Sargent, whose name appears so frequently in the last chapter. We went together very often to witness these manifestations, and they interested him very much, more than any other phase, unless it was that of independent slate-writing. I might add that that distinguished *litterateur* and scholar was always more interested in the sensuous class of manifestations than in the sometimes-called higher phases of the mental, ethical, or trance descriptions. One can see this preference by reading his publications,— " The Planchette," or " The Scientific Basis of Spiritualism."

I am also similarly inclined, with Mr. Sargent, for a preference for the sensuous, but am as much interested in the intellectual also, because I am in those of a sensuous or phenomenal character. If the phenomenal or the sensuous were eliminated, the other, and may be higher, phases in the minds of many would not stand as spiritual manifestations if unsupported by the former. The fact that raps are made, and movements of material objects without material contact, and other descriptions of physical phenomena so clearly manifest by an intelligent invisible power, or what I have called sensuous proof, it throws a luster of truth, or, at least, a luster of reasonableness on the other, of which the observation, unaided by the sensuous phases, would not detect any super-mundane source for the other, or trance or inspirational utterances. They would, unaided by the sensuous, all be considered normal qualities,—

hardly explainable, to be sure, as founded on education, but nothing more than is noticeable all over the world in the realm of thought and oratory.

With a knowledge of the fact that comes so distinctly in the sensuous phases of this impulse, force, or power, it explains very rationally some extraordinary gifts in quite uneducated people, indicating a royal road of information and knowledge, besides being independent of a scholastic one, and goes still farther than that, extending the principle over the mentality of mankind, whether Spiritualists or not.

All thoughtful people on this subject, and favoring it, consider it of a natural and not a supernatural character; therefore, there is a law for it, and, if there is, "this divinity that shapes our ends," of which Shakespeare fancifully spoke, and which modern Spiritualism teaches under a more modest name, this supervision or influence, whether we believe it or not, reaches all human beings, and many an oration that is a masterpiece of intellectual and eloquent effort may date more or less from a higher source than the utterer of it, teaching us that there are Davids, Ezekiels, Isaiahs, and St. Pauls today in the various walks of life as there were in the days of old.

It is possible that the Lulu Hursts, or other magnetically-strong people today, may teach us without drawing on the supernatural how Sampson was able to do what he did in his day, if he did, as recorded. It seems to me, also, the poets, from Homer down to Holmes, as Thoreau has said: "Keeping in advance of the glare of philosophy, always dwelling in an auroral atmosphere, writing glowing and ruddy fables that precede the noonday thoughts of men as aurora does the sun's rays." Certainly, if one wants to find profound truths in harmony with modern Spiritualism, and not intending any such harmony only as a pleasing fancy, he will find them in abundance in the writings of the poets.

Under the thought which I have expressed, I am inclined to think when the poets, in this auroral state of mind, write, as the bard of Avon did, when he said : —

> "As imagination bodies forth
> The forms of things unknown, the poet's pen
> Turns them to shape, and gives to airy nothing
> A local habitation and a name,"

they will find that they had not been building castles in the air, but will find often that they are proving what that great scholar Henry Thomas Buckle said: "That the imagination of the poet in one age forecasts the discoveries of science in the next;" and then cited many pages of instances to prove it, just as modern Spiritualism has been making literal truth many of the poetical beauties of Longfellow, and of many other well-remembered poets.

I began this chapter with the intention of relating some of Colchester's manifestations, and I think I will not change my mind, but let what I have said answer for an introduction, or a setting to them. His manifestations were various in kind. He had the red letters of initials and names of departed friends come on his arms; he gave tests also with pellets, and many other forms of the phenomena.

The phase most interesting to Epes Sargent, as well as to me, was the artistic execution of pictures on cards with colored pencils or crayons, without any manipulation or mechanical action, the execution being by will-power, and, it is reasonable to say, by the spirits. I will describe an instance by way of illustration : —

We were seated around a table at the pleasant home of Daniel Farrar, of Hancock Street, Boston. The table was about four feet by two, square. There were six persons making this circle, consisting of Mr. and Mrs. Farrar, Mrs. Wetherbee, Epes Sargent, myself, and Colchester,— two on each of the long sides, and one each on the ends. I had an end seat, and the back of my chair was against the bureau that was on the side of the room, and Sargent was my *vis-a-vis*. We were having a very satisfactory time, with a variety of manifestations, and the circle was a remarkably good one.

Colchester said to me : "Take a few of those plain, white cards" (they were on the table for the purpose) "and put them in one of the drawers back of you, marking them first so as to know them again." I did so, cutting a crooked piece out of the corner of each, and retaining them for the purpose. There were six in number of the cards that I took and put in the drawer. "Now, take a handful of those crayons," said he, "and throw them in, and shut the drawer." It may be well to say that the drawer was quite full of white, folded cotton materials, leaving no spare room, so that the cards and pencils were in tolerably close quarters.

We proceeded then with the manifestations as before, and in perhaps about half an hour, in which we had other manifestations, Mr. Colchester said to me: "Better now open the drawer, and see how the cards look." I got up, and had to, as before, in order to move my chair so as to open the drawer, and took out what were once the six clean, white cards, and found a picture, artistically drawn, on each of them, —flowers, fruit, landscapes, birds, etc.,—and the colors used in the pictures thus drawn were the colors of the crayons or pencils that were put in the bureau drawer. Those crayons that we left on the table were not expressed in the pictures. I hardly need to say that this was done in a brightly-lighted room, and nobody had any access to the drawer, and could not if they had desired to, as I was sitting so closely to it, and had to move my chair before I could open it.

It would take much time to write out in detail all my experiences with this medium. I will add one other experience,—one of many,—it was certainly very remarkable.

One day when Epes Sargent and I were going to attend one of his seances, at the same gentleman's house, he said to me: "Suppose you stop at some store on your way there, and buy some white paste-board,—the cards used are all right enough, but, with our own, it will make the statement stronger, if we should ever want to make one,"—and I did so; and, before the seance began, cut this purchased pasteboard into pieces about six inches square, so had about a dozen of them, which I laid in a pile on the table that we were going to use.

This time — and usually the seance was in Mr. Farrar's parlor — we used there an extension-table, and, on this occasion, about a dozen of us were seated around it, Mr. Colchester sitting next to me. After having much writing on papers or pellets, and many pictures drawn in this inscrutable way, Mr. Colchester said to me: "Take one of your pieces of card, Mr. Wetherbee, and mark it so that you will know it again, and pass it to me." I did so, cutting off a crooked piece on the corner, and putting it in my pocket, and passed the mutilated card, clean and white, to him. He took it with his thumb and finger and shied it over into the opposite corner of the room, grabbed up a handful of the crayons that were on the table, and threw them over altogether into the corner where the card had been shied, saying, at the same time: "Go and pick the card up;" and I did so, and found an artistically-drawn picture on it.

In the execution of this picture, all the colors that the crayons were composed of were used, and which lay, as they had fallen, helter-skelter about that corner of the room. The piece of it that I had kept in my pocket as a detector fitted the mutilation exactly, and the fact of its being the same identical piece of cardboard was unmistakable. This was not a solitary experiment; there were many of them, and often, but one instance is enough to relate. You will readily see that this was not, and could not, have been a mechanical experiment.

On one of these occasions, during the experiment of writing the names of departed spirits on pellets, this circumstance occurred. It also was not a solitary instance; but one is enough to mention. Colchester said to Mr. Farrar: "Now write a few names on some slips of paper, and fix one of them in your mind, without showing them to me, and go and throw them out of the window;" and Mr. Farrar did so. "Now," said he, "think of that name, and tell me where you would like to find it." Remember, the pellets were thrown out of the window, and were somewhere out on Hancock Street, blowing wherever the wind chose to waft them.

Being thus asked where he would like to find the pellet with the special name on it, Mr. Farrar said: "In the first vase on the mantel-shelf" (there were three vases there). He went to the vase and found a pellet there. "Do not open it," said Colchester; but he took a piece of paper and wrote a name, and when the pellet was opened by Mr. Farrar it was the same as written by Colchester, and was the name Mr. Farrar had in his mind, and seemed to be one of those that had been thrown out of the window; at any rate, it was one written by Mr. Farrar, and he wrote no others but the batch he threw, by request, out of the window. Epes Sargent, Hon. Charles E.

Jenkins, as well as myself and others, all had the same opportunities, with the same success.

At some of these seances of Mr. Colchester's, at the house of Mr. Farrar, there was present an interesting French lady, of middle age. She was a stranger to all but the Farrars, and had not been long in this country. This lady had lost a daughter a few weeks before she left Paris. She was a very spiritual-looking and talking lady, and became very much interested in Spiritualism, and what she received at these seances, and the way she expressed herself, made everything she got as interesting to us or the others as if personal to themselves.

There had been a great many pictures made on this occasion. White cards were placed in a pile on the floor, and a number of crayons on them, about four feet from the medium. Each card in the pile was marked severally by each one of the circle, and the pile and the crayons were covered over with a table-cloth to insure darkness, and there was a picture found at short intervals on each, so that each person got one,—all executed without human manipulation or mechanical power.

This French lady was then told to take one of the plain, white pieces of cardboard, and hold it under the table. The hands of all present, including the medium's, were in plain sight on the table. In a few minutes the French lady was requested to lay the card she was holding under the table on the table for inspection. There was found upon it a picture and a communication. I will try and describe it.

Near the center was a circle drawn on it, around the
outside of which was a wreath of flowers. Inside of
this circle was written a very affectionate message
to the lady, signed with the name of her departed
daughter who had died, as has been mentioned, a few
weeks before she left Paris. The writing was so
neat and small it could with difficulty be read except
with a magnifying-glass.

No one knew anything about the circumstances of
this lady except the Farrars, and they only the circumstances named, and that she was an entire stranger
to the medium. This, then, all things considered,
was one of the most perfect tests of intelligent spirit
power and spirit presence, and even of identification,
that one could possibly have.

When relating this incident once in a newspaper
article, I closed it with the quotation of a line or two
of poetry; and now, wanting to put a finish to this
long chapter, I will do so with the same lines, which
are as follows : —

> "It may be
> The thoughts that visit us — we know not whence —
> Sudden as inspiration, are the whispers
> Of disembodied spirits, speaking to us
> As friends, who wait outside a prison wall,
> Through the barred windows speak to those within."

" I am ready to admit that the heart cries out for love just as loudly as the brain calls for law ; and, further, I am ready to admit that to gain order for the head at the price of the loss of happiness and trust for the heart is a most questionable advantage, or even a positive loss ; for the heart and its needs are as real and as true and high a part of human life as is the knowledge and thought of the brain. I even believe that happiness and peace are so necessary a part of life that any life is a failure that in the long run does not gain them."— *Rev. M. J. Savage.*

93

VIII.

PHANTOMATIC TABLE-TALK.

Being an article illustrative of the subject in general.

There are some things said in the following article which I wrote for and was printed in the *Boston Commonwealth*, that are worth mentioning in this book, and will help incidentally to throw a luster on some of its preceding and succeeding pages. I am aware that part of it is superfluous in this connection, but I think I had better present it without any mutilation. The reader can skip whatever seems to him irrelevant : —

There it stands in the opposite corner of the room, looking at me; and yet how can a table without eyes look at one? But I have reason to think that it once did see me; yes, and many times, or apparently did, and perhaps it does now. But this needs an explanation, and would perhaps be more properly expressed if I said an invisible presence, acting through it, made this piece of furniture seem to see me, or act as if it did.

I am speaking of a small, old-fashioned table, or lightstand, which was made in 1751. That was the year that Gray gave to the world his immortal "Elegy." I did not know that fact once in this connection, but this old table once told me so itself, and the encyclopædia indorsed the statement. What a story this old table could tell — now one hundred and thirty-three years old — if it were only sentient and vocal!

Why should I say "if," after making the above historic statement as voiced by the table? If Robert Southey could address a mummy whose cerements had not been disturbed for three thousand years, and make it poetically vocal, so may I address this table and make it vocal. I think I have the advantage of the poet as to the facts in the case, but that is a matter which will be brought out as I proceed.

Even now, as I am looking at the old table, and the large, old Bible resting on it, of the same age, — for the title-page of that shows it was printed in MDCCLI., — how in fancy the old familiar ancestral faces are associated with them, — table and book; these, by some affinity, have always stuck by each other. In their connection, in my mind's eye, how plainly I see the venerable face of my grandmother, who used to explain the quaint old pictures to my youthful mind, and her sister also (my mother's aunt) often in the same instructive occupation, and (using a line from Robert Burns) like

"The father, mixing a' wi' admonition due."

This latter relative of mine, when she ascended, was ninety-three years old, and she was born also in 1751.

What a year 1751 must have been to the tribe of
"Shadows"! This old table came into form, the
old Bible resting on it was printed, that same year;
and in 1751 that old relative, Aunt Fales, was born;
and, as I have said, Gray's "Elegy" was published.
Am I straining a point in associating this poem with
what is only personal property? Well, let us see.

That piece of immortal literature has nothing to do
with this old table, or with the Bible on it, or with
my venerable relative; and yet an incident of an
Endoric character in its connection makes the poem
a feature in this quadrangular picture. Irrespective
of the incident referred to, I find an association
between it and my thought in one of its verses. Let
me quote it: —

> "There at the foot of yonder nodding beech,
> That wreathes its old fantastic roots so high,
> His listless length at noontide would he stretch,
> And pore upon the brook that babbles by."

Am I not, even if not prone, poring on the table
that "babbles by"? I am quite literal, as well as
phantomatic, when I say "babble." But I may as
well relate the Endoric incident which gives me more
than a poetic connection with Gray's "Elegy," and
explain at the same time the significance of "babble,"
and perhaps add a solemn luster to the matter on
which I am writing.

A woman was once living with me in the capacity
of nurse. Accidentally, both to her and myself, I
found that she possessed that constitutional quality
that some people have, that in their presence, and

sometimes without contact, as was the case with this young woman, inanimate tables and other objects become animate, and intelligently move, it would seem, by the said objects' own volition, or give off audible sounds, or raps, as they are called, that are intelligent, and as translatable as a ticker in a telegraph office. This old table was particularly apt to be thus talkative, when near enough to this woman to be within the sphere of her magnetism.

This person lived with us about two years, and I thus had two years of very valuable experience. She was not aware she had this power until I discovered it, and she knew nothing at first of my dead and buried relatives; but noticing this phenomenon, and investigating it with this old table, to her surprise and mine the translation of the sounds and movements by the alphabet proved to be communications from individuals who had died.

This was no surprise to me, because I had had experience before, but I was a little surprised to find one of the invisibles giving the name of " Hannah," particularly when in reply to "Hannah who?" the response came "Fales,"—for that was Aunt Fales, the old relative who was born in 1751. The moment I recognized her the table was violently active, as if to express pleasant emotion at the recognition. I was sure, under the circumstances, that I was in the presence of my departed relative, whose body had long before been laid away in the grave.

This was no solitary instance. The manifestations during those two years were multitudinous, and of every variety. I do not propose now to make any record of them in detail, but will mention one instance in connection with this relative, because her birth-year and this table's and Bible's birth-year were the same. I have other reasons, also, which will explain themselves as I proceed.

It was at one of these Endoric interviews (I use the word "Endoric," because during my life a picture in that old book of the woman of Endor raising Samuel was one that had often attracted her attention, and of course mine), as if to prove an intelligence that was distinct from and superior to the young woman's through whose influence this old table was thus vocal, and possibly to make the point certain that the information did not come from me by mind-reading, that the table-raps claiming to be from Aunt Fales said this table and Bible and Gray's "Elegy" were of the same age. As I have said, investigation showed me that the poem was published in 1751. So this old table, or the invisible intelligence using it as a mouthpiece, was a well-read institution, and also had told the truth.

A little argument will seem to be in order here: That poem then, as now, was very popular, and all intelligent people, a hundred years ago, were familiar with it; the world was not then as full as it is now of good productions, hence the minds of the thoughtful were not as crowded as they are now; and so in this case the poem, being probably as familiar to her as the Lord's Prayer, came readily to the surface, when such a circumstance today might be called pedantry. Everyone will remember that General Wolfe, the hero of the successful battle on the Heights of Abraham, declared admiringly that he would rather be the author of that poem than the winner of battles.

Speaking now of the communication, and the coincidence of the date, which I knew nothing about in any definite manner, it was a felicity in thought that I appreciate, and I have no doubt the spirit of Aunt Fales did, too; and if that woman (I mean the nurse) were now alive, and present at this moment, I have no doubt this old table would signify its knowledge of what I am writing about by a visible manifestation sufficient to joggle the old book that now rests on it. But, old table, though you are now still, I feel that the presence is there; and so I will say, as the poet said when lately speaking of Burns: —

> "A presence haunts this room tonight,
> A force of mingled mist and light,
>   From that far coast.
> Welcome beneath this roof of mine!
> Welcome! this vacant chair is thine,
>   Dear friend and ghost!"

I am writing very truthfully, and not drawing at all on my imagination. This being admitted, is not this incident pretty good evidence that this venerable lady of 1751 was still alive and at this table at that time, and possibly now? Certainly some one was, for a table cannot speak unaided; and if anyone was, it may as likely have been she as another. Does it not almost make the tender fancy of Longfellow,

when he speaks of the departed, as something more
than poetry,—something actual? This, for instance,
may be wiser than he knew : —

> " There are more guests at table than the hosts
>   Invited.   This illumined hall
>   Is thronged with quiet, inoffensive ghosts
>   As silent as the pictures on the wall."

Though alone now in my library, I do not feel that
I am alone. Looking at that table and its associations, I almost feel, aided perhaps by my imagination, "a sense of something moving to and fro."
One of my ancestors was a seeress,— could at times
see the forms of the departed, and knew them, and
sometimes knew their wishes and intentions. As
this ancestor was, during her earthly life, the owner
of both table and Bible, she may, in a sentimental
sense, still hold the fee of them.

To be understood, let me quote again a verse from
the same poet, which expresses the idea better and
briefer than I otherwise can : —

> " We have no title-deeds to house or lands ;
>   Owners and occupants of earlier dates
>   From graves forgotten stretch their dusky hands,
>   And hold in *mortmain* still their old estates."

She may have lent to these venerable articles a
charm that lingers, and, in a sentimental way, influences her descendant, inspiring his thought, as the
subject certainly does; but memories of those ancients
out of the form, these old mementoes still in the
form, crowd upon me thick and fast, and for fear of

being too lengthy for a newspaper article, I think I had better turn off the gas, so to speak, or rather the flow of ink; so, with the relation of an interesting circumstance which old Aunt Fales has often told me, I will close this article.

This, to be sure, will not be an item of "phantomatic table-talk," as I relate it from memory, but it always interested me, and may be interesting to others, as it is a fact in early Boston history; and the old table, though at this moment voiceless, seems to invite me to do what it could of itself if the old conditions were now attainable.

Abiel Smith, who was Aunt Fales's brother, lived on State Street, at the corner of Pudding Lane, now Devonshire Street. This was before the war of the Revolution. His store, where he and his wife had done a thrifty business for some years, was on the ground floor; over it, and in the rear, the family lived. He had no children, so his family were his wife and the shop-tenders,— who were generally his relatives,— male and female, from the country. Times had become warlike and troublesome,— the English soldiers were encamped on the Neck, and ingress and egress to and from the town were difficult, and, under the circumstances, rather dangerous.

Aunt Fales, then a young woman, was living with them at this period. Her sister-in-law, Mrs. Smith, began to feel uneasy about their property, and wanted to get out of the city with it; but Abiel saw that that was impossible. She proposed a division, and she would try to take care of her half. They made a fair division,—on the one side, the debts and the stock, and, perhaps, the house; and on the other, the gold. Mrs. Smith took the gold, which was about $20,000, for her part, leaving her husband the more valuable half, but, of course, the more risky half. Mrs. Smith and Aunt Fales then made some petticoats and quilted a guinea in every square, and when the two women were dressed for their journey they had $20,000 in gold in their skirts. In that way they rode through the British lines.

In their agitation, Mrs. Smith could not find the key of their trunk, and the inspecting soldier broke it open with his bayonet, and, finding nothing contraband, let them pass through the lines. Aunt Fales said she never was so frightened in all her life; but they got safely out into the country, gold and all. When the British evacuated, as they did a few months after, Mrs. Smith returned with her gold. It was a matter of some surprise among the merchants of those days where "old Smith" got so much money, for he became a larger buyer of goods, and always had the "ready" to pay for his purchases.

This was the beginning of one of the large fortunes of those times, and Abiel Smith, who survived his wife a year or two, died early in this century, and, having no children, his large fortune, for those days, was divided among his relatives, chiefly the sons and daughters of his eleven brothers and sisters.

IX.

Some description of him, and experiences he and the writer have had together. — Joseph Cook.

> " My sprightly neighbor, gone before,
>   To that unknown and silent shore,
>   Shall we not meet as heretofore,
>   Some summer morning? "

I commence with this quotation a chapter on my friend and neighbor, Epes Sargent, not because it in any sense applies to him, but because he has often quoted it as applicable to me, strained possibly, and also as an illustration in his many conferences with me. Although it is some of the "jubilant spray" from Charles Lamb's flow of cheerful thought, I always think of it in connection with our late scholarly brother, Epes Sargent.

How many times and how pleasantly has the calm face of this friend and neighbor shone in upon me while seated in my library room reading or writing, as I am now. He could see me very plainly as he came down the street past my library window, and then, walking in, would spend a few minutes, and sometimes an hour or two, in pleasant conversation on the subject of the spirits, in which we were both so interested.

I do not say this for the sake of telling of our intellectual intimacy, and the open and free manner he communicated with me, sometimes reading a manuscript of some book, or part of one, that he was preparing for the press. Two or three of his later works I knew something of in the composition of them by this familiar ante-natal inspection.

I am now writing a chapter under his name as the subject, and who knows but by his invisible direction? I am sure it is by his influence. I can say that much without encroaching upon the domain of the super-mundane. I feel that anything I have to say of our cultured friend will find a hospitable reception from the readers of this book, which, I suppose, will generally be Spiritualists, or the philo-spiritual class; for though the intellectual stars now shining in our firmament of thought are many and notable compared with the earlier days of the cause, Epes Sargent, as editor, poet, scholar, and *litterateur* was conspicuous, and a credit to this fast-rising and spreading light.

I have known him as townsman and neighbor a great many years, from a comparatively young man to a somewhat old one,—that is, if a man is old when he is in the sixties. I saw, however, much more of him during his last decade than at any earlier period of his life, our similarity of thought drawing us into closer intellectual communion.

I was somewhat informed of his last book, "The
Scientific Basis of Spiritualism," in advance of its
publication, and it was with much pleasure I said
"Yea, verily," to him when he presented me a copy,
and said he would be glad for me to give in print my
opinion of it. I said to Mr. Sargent: "I will do so
with pleasure, but you know my way of presenting a
thing is very different from your way. You are scholarly and methodic, and I make no pretensions to the
literary guild. I am, you know, a Bohemian in the
pen line, though well-behaved morally." "I want
you," said he in reply, "to express yourself in your
own way. I would prefer your sincerity, warmth,
and naturalness to any closet production from what
you call scholarly people."

As I have an interesting reminiscence to relate
before passing from his name in this connection, I
will copy a paragraph or two from my article on his
last book, both as an introduction to the reminiscence referred to and also as a fact in current literary life, showing the sacrifices a man even of established reputation makes by identifying himself with
this subject.

This, however, is somewhat passing away, and the
fact that a popular metropolitan minister, like the
Rev. M. J. Savage, can say, and have it widely
reported as he did in a late Easter-Sunday sermon:
"Modern Spiritualism is too big a fact in modern life
to be ignored; thousands and thousands in Europe
and America believe in its central claim. There are
thousands of silent believers also who do not like to

be called knave or fool, and so keep still about it, and, like Nicodemus, they come by night, lest they be cast out of the synagogue." It shows, as he says, it is too large a matter now to be ignored.

The paragraph referred to that I propose to copy from the old article of which I have spoken, reads as follows : —

" As plenty as books are, it is no ordinary thing when a man of thought and culture, who has a hearing, writes a book on a subject that has had his careful study and investigation for a score or two of years, and especially when, as in the matter before us, after these pains and study, he writes a book on an unpopular subject, a subject avoided by the leading minds of the age, because prejudice and fashion are against it, because no credit is to be gained by the effort in its behalf in the world of letters; in fact, when the history of its investigation has shown without an exception that no amount of erudition, or reputation for wisdom, no successes in other fields of literary or scientific pursuits on their part, have been sufficient to secure for its witnesses a respectful or respectable hearing in the aristocracy of letters; or, putting it in the mildest form, any favorable report, or any defense of the subject on the ground of its basis of truth, or its worthiness of attention.— the verdict has been in each case by his fellow-*savants*, that the man thus bearing witness to the unpopular fact is in his dotage. or getting credulous as he grows old, or has been duped by imposition in fields where he was not expert.

"A book, then, on this subject 'with the image and superscription of Cæsar upon it,' so to speak, is an extraordinary thing, and should be welcomed by the body politic of Spiritualists, and also, to some extent, by the educated outside world, who are so apt to think that nothing good comes out of Nazareth.

"The history of every scholar, or man of established reputation, who has become more or less identified with or has defended modern Spiritualism, will warrant the assertion I have made, and that in a popular sense the 'Light' in literature and science who undertakes its investigation, if fair and honest, has everything to lose and nothing to gain, except the consoling fact of its truth.

"If a man is in eclipse on account of it today, his shining hour will arrive sometime, at least in the hereafter, and this especial truth being the perpetuity of individual conscious life beyond the grave, the consolation referred to is a compensation in a very peculiar sense."

The reminiscences to which I have referred, and considering what I have said and quoted in the light of an introduction, is as follows : —

It was a short time, perhaps a week, after I had attended Mr. Sargent's funeral, that I was sitting at the writing-table in my library, pen in hand, calculating to work on a matter that I had put off until then, and was proposing to devote the evening to it. My eye accidentally fell on the lines with which I began this chapter. They were in my scrap-book;

they had a red-pencil mark against them, as if at some previous time they had made an impression upon me. At that moment they seemed to speak to me as if there really was a man or a spirit back of them, and I have a strong impression there was.

I read them, and thinking of Epes Sargent who had then so lately deceased, I said aloud, as if in response to the Lamb lines: "Yes, of course, we will!" I seemed to feel that he was speaking to me those words, as he had done when he was alive and talking with me. Only a few weeks before that evening he was sitting opposite me at this table where I am now writing. He spent, as he often had, an hour or so with me in social converse,—getting the news, as he called it,—as he lived more in the closet than I did, I living more in the world of affairs, so we could change our center of gravity and be mutually beneficial.

I had a very strong feeling that he was sitting there then as an invisible spirit,—there was the same soft chair that he occupied then as a visible one. I often feel the presence of unseen company in this way when I am alone. Longfellow expresses my thought in this connection better than I can, so I will quote the verse, and I did audibly at the time of which I am speaking:—

> "His presence haunts this room tonight,
> A force of mingled mist and light
>   From that far coast.
> Welcome beneath this roof of mine!
> Welcome! this vacant chair is thine,
>   Dear friend and ghost!"

Referring to the lines again of Charles Lamb, which set my pen in motion at the time in this direction, instead of doing the work that I was intending to do, "Sprightly" hardly applies to our late "guest and ghost," for he was the reverse of that; he was genial, but very solid and thoughtful; so far also from my being sprightly, I have wondered what he found to appreciate in me, for by the application of my being his "sprightly neighbor," and he was my sedate and thoughtful one. I do not claim the cognomen; I only mention it because he has expressed an interest in my peculiar way of saying things, which, as everyone knows, is quite the reverse of his way. He was scholarly and very careful,—I am only natural.

I appreciated his able additions to spiritual literature. How thankful we all ought to be that, with his prestige of literary standing, he so identified himself with Spiritualism.

I had one or two sittings with Susan Nickerson White, the late well-known medium, within a week or two after his decease, one of them the next day after his funeral, not for the purpose of communicating with him, but for another object entirely, and one or two during the subsequent week or two. I will give a brief sketch of them where they refer to him. They interested me as being worthy of record, so that I now do not wholly draw on my memory, and yet the circumstances are very distinct there also.

Mr. Sargent's funeral was on Sunday. On the next afternoon I had a sitting, as I have said, with

Mrs. White. She said, before going into a trance: "I see a man by the side of you; he is a small man; hair thin and gray, and head a little bald; he puts his hand on your head." The medium then became entranced, and said with a slow, low, and distinct voice: "Wetherbee, you can hardly realize it, but I am Epes Sargent." I did realize it, and felt from the first, when clairvoyantly she said she saw and described the small man standing near me, that it was Epes Sargent. He then, in the same low and distinct voice, quite different from the medium's in her normal state, spoke of his change, how he found things as he expected, and so would I, he said: "It is just the place that we used to expect it would be."

In the pause that followed, thinking of his funeral that I had attended the day before, I remarked to him that I was glad that Spiritualism was not ignored at his funeral services. "Yes," he replied, "William spoke well, did he not?—I mean Mr. William Mountford." The spirit seemed to correct himself after saying William, for I did not know the reverend gentleman's name by William, but he, being an old friend of Mr. Mountford, it was natural for him to say William, but it required the Mountford for me to know to whom he referred. I was aware of and pleased with the funeral address by him, and so, in reply to the spirit said: "Yes, he did speak well." After talking in this way a little while, the spirit said: "I could not resist the opportunity of coming to you at this time, but as you are here, Wetherbee, for other matters, I will take my leave, for your friends are already waiting to talk with you."

I think I have very good reason to think this was Epes Sargent's spirit. Mrs. White told me afterwards that she did not know Mr. Sargent only by reputation; never saw him in her life that she knew of. Most people who knew me as well as Mr. Sargent did would call me John when addressing me; but Sargent always called me Wetherbee, and omitting the "Mr."; and it will be noticed on this occasion that the medium, or the spirit rather, so addressed me. It rather seems to me, if there had been a pretence, at this time it would have been safer to have said John (for a spirit is privileged to take liberties) than to have called me Wetherbee, and though it is only a straw it shows the direction of the wind.

At a subsequent sitting, Mr. Sargent came in the same modest way, only using a very little of the time, but enough to let me know that he was my "guest and ghost" at my home, leading me to infer from what he did say that he had influenced the change of work or thought on the evening of which I have spoken, where the Lamb-stanza so sentimentally hove in sight, as the mariner would say. There is nothing certain about this as there is about some of my experiences, for the fact was very strongly in my mind that Epes Sargent was concerned in the cogitation of which I have spoken, and a spirit might have reached it from me on the principle of mind-reading; but, believing as I do, what is the use of straining for a negative solution? It pleases me whether it does anybody else or not. I give his presence the benefit of the doubt.

A JOSEPH COOK REMINISCENCE.

While presenting this article under the heading of Epes Sargent, I may as well add to it a page or two in relation to the Rev. Joseph Cook, in connection with him, referring to his investigation of the phenomena at Mr. Sargent's house. I hardly need to say that I am no hero worshiper, and am very apt to think that one man is about equal to another in one sense, or, at least, in the absolute sense; but there are some people who, from luck, ability, or circumstances have a prestige or prominence among their fellows, so that what they say or do has more effect, gets a wider hearing, carrying with it an influence more than the average.

A suggestive statement may be made by a nobody, so to speak, the utterer an obscure individual, and but little attention given to it; but the same statement uttered by a Wendell Phillips, or other notable, and it gets a hearing from one end of the country to the other. It is an idea of this kind that leads me to speak of Joseph Cook in this connection. He seems to have become (or had in the day of which I am now speaking) one of the prominent evangelical lights, giving a course or two of lectures in the Old South Church, in Boston, which was a feature in the religious doings of that city.

His utterances were so sensational as well as bright, aiming, or claiming also, to make modern science and religion coalesce or harmonize, that his discourses, reported in full in the respectable dailies, were read by a million people, and furnished the thought for half the evangelical pulpits in New England. He, therefore, is one of the prominent men whose sayings and doings were of more consequence than any hundred perhaps of equally able men. This, then, is the reason why I think what I have to say of his investigation a matter of more than passing notice.

After Mr. Sargent had received from me the perfect evidence I had had of spirit-writing, and having gone himself, and under somewhat remarkable circumstances, got the communication that was so self-satisfying, he followed it up, giving a good deal of attention to Mr. Watkins's phenomenon, and it was frequently given at his own house, and he and his family had great proof of the perfect genuineness of the manifestations. I have before me now a long communication of his that was printed in the *Boston Transcript*, full of such convincing points and detailed statements that anyone believing the testimony of Epes Sargent, the scholarly author of the "Scientific Basis of Spiritualism," could not help believing in modern Spiritualism. Some of them are worth repeating here, but having in my mind the Cook investigation, I think I had better confine myself to that.

Mr. Sargent, learning that Mr. Cook would like to. witness some of the phenomena with Watkins in some respectable way, a seance was arranged for his benefit. This was on March 13, 1880. In speaking of it afterwards at the next Monday's lecture to his large audience in the Old South, he began with these words (I copy them from the report in the *Boston Advertiser*) : —

"In the library of Epes Sargent, last Saturday, I consented to see a psychic, of whom I had heard various things, some of them not altogether reassuring. I took with me my family physician (laughter) and my wife (laughter and applause). In the company of nine persons assembled in the library there were four believers and five unbelievers in Spiritualism."

He then gave the details of the experiments, saying where they were satisfactory and where they were unsatisfactory. There were many points of each. A careful reading of each of these departments will show to any fair-minded man that the satisfactory points were in no way impaired by the reading of the unsatisfactory ones. I suppose they were qualifications, or loop-holes, for partial retreat. should he be hurting his usefulness or popularity by his admissions. The paper signed by all present, including Joseph Cook, speaks for itself, and is all any Spiritualist asks of an outsider, " that fraud does not account for it ; " the solution will take care of itself. Here is a copy of the document that Joseph Cook and the others signed : —

"At the house of Epes Sargent, on the evening of Saturday, March 13, 1880, the undersigned saw two clean slates placed face to face, with a bit of slate-pencil between them.

We all held our hands clasped around the edges of the two slates. Mr. Watkins's hands also clasped the slates.

"In this position, we all distinctly heard the pencil moving, and on opening the slates found an intelligent message, in a strong, masculine hand, in answer to a question asked by one of the company.

"Afterwards, two slates were clamped together with strong brass fixtures, and held at arm's length by Mr. Cook, while the rest of the company and the psychic had their hands in full view on the table. After a moment of waiting, the slates were opened, and a message, in a feminine hand, was found on one of the inner surfaces. There were five lighted gas-burners in the room at the time.

"We cannot apply to these facts any theory of fraud, and we do not see how the writing can be explained, unless matter in the slate-pencil was moved without contact."

The paper, of which the above is an exact copy, signed by Mr. Cook and the others, speaks for itself. Mr. Sargent often spoke to me of this seance, and the circumstances, and said Mr. Cook was very much pleased and interested in what he saw, and came to him at starting, saying: "I thank you, Mr. Sargent, for the opportunity of seeing the manifestations under such favorable circumstances; the back-bone of materialism is broken." I am very particular in the wording of this parting statement, and know I have got it exactly right, for Mr. Sargent mentioned it to me at least four times that I distinctly remember.

X.

ON LEANNESS OF THOUGHT.

The deficiency is made up by the sensuous proof of a spiritual source.

There is much in current Spiritualism that violates the taste of cultured, intellectual people, at least those outside of our ranks. The phenomenal, or sensuous, phases in themselves lack dignity, especially as in dealing with them we are dealing with the dead. The intellectual or ethical phases, also, are lean as mental efforts, especially when attributed to departed people of celebrity.

In making this remark I have the latter phase more especially in my mind. The source adds luster to the sensuous, irrespective of its quality of thought, as being instructive or entertaining. Crabs, scorpions, goats, and fishes become sublime when hung up as signs of the zodiac, says Emerson; and, in like manner, do table-tippings, and grotesque movements of ponderable bodies become sublime when such movements are signs of invisible intelligence.

So does the source fatten any leanness in the intellectual phase; but the source in the latter is not so self-evident as is the sensuous class. There is often so little bread to so much sack, when looked at from an outside standpoint. So many communications or discourses coming from the vanished stars of intellect, or historic lights, that show a shrinkage of ability, that it often occurs to me, or, rather, it is often said to me, is the product worth all the trouble? Wading through slaughter to a throne, is the throne of the truth when reached worthy of the struggle? Is the button of value valuable enough to compensate for the handling of so much scoria, or base metal? I think it is, for it supplies a human need, a necessity, and it cannot be found outside of the subject; but, finding it, it casts a luster outside and beyond itself, and brings to the front and into notice valuable lore, — truth that would otherwise remain in the domain of fancy, fable, or disease.

Experiencing what I have, and the leanness of much of that experience, I never blame anyone from falling by the way and giving up the struggle, looking a little ways, then retreating, as Prof. Tyndall did, and as Prof. Crookes did not. Both of these *savants* were satisfied, it seems, one in one way, and one in the other.

I have nothing to do with superficial examinations of an affair, or with people who presume they have encompassed it, when I know they have not. I am only too thankful that my first experience was such an unmistakable clincher as to sustain me, in this desert of thought, if one chooses to call it so, until I reached another oasis, and so it has ever been.

A circumstance in my domestic life, lasting for nearly two years, coming at an opportune time, seems to have been all that I needed to make my affirmative convictions enduring, even if one chooses to consider it, as I have said, among the average leanness of its current thought. The momentum obtained from the circumstance referred to would have been sufficient had the "Gates Ajar" been forever thereafter closed to have kept me constant in the line of its thought. Of this, more will be said hereafter.

One cannot help noticing the manifest relative weakness of the thought that comes from the spiritual Channings and Parkers, the Shakespeares and the Miltons, compared to their utterances when they were in the form. They are often, however, masterpieces of good intellectual work for the instruments uttering the thoughts, who are often people without education. I remember once a young lady, conspicuous now on the spiritual platform, who was present at a friend's house, where the parlors were filled with intelligent and cultured people, some of them eminently so; and an erudite and difficult subject was given to this young trance-speaker to address them upon; and it was a remarkable discourse, eloquent, finished, and logical. That it would have been a creditable effort for most anyone, the following colloquy will show: —

C. C. Felton, the then professor, afterwards president, of Harvard College, who was one of the listeners on that occasion, congratulated her on the dis-

course, and added, rather pleasantly: "Now, own up
and say it was yourself, and take the credit that
would belong to you as one of the most cultivated
ladies of the country." She replied to him: "I
would be very glad to, if it was only true; but I do
not claim it as my effort; I know it was not myself,
for I know nothing of the subject." I do not think
Prof. Felton believed her, but I did, for I knew well
the history or circumstances of her life.

For all that, and similar inspirational addresses,
most of the utterances made by the departed intellectual lights through living organisms, as I have said,
show a great falling off in quality, that, judging from
a human standpoint, the parties, if in the form them
selves, would be ashamed of their productions, and
would never have uttered them; and from such a
standpoint it is reasonable to suppose they never did,
and allowing their thought to partake of the channel,
the brain of the medium being used by such a spirit
with its deficiencies, so as to convey it in bad gram-
mar and lack of characteristic finish, even if the
thought be in harmony, such a spirit would hardly
allow his thought to go abroad in such an ill dress.

It would seem as if the dictating spirit can only
know it as he expresses it, presuming it issues into
mortal hearing as he gives it out, not perceiving its
outcome in the mundane sphere. This can hardly be
the case, though it is possible. Of course there are
grand and eminent exceptions to this watering of
thought, but enough of the deficiencies are noticeable
to make the claim a subject of criticism, especially

among those who view it superficially, or from the outside, and have never looked into the philosophy or the dynamics of the subject only as a passing affair.

I have spoken of a domestic circumstance. Now, to be more explicit, one of the most fruitful periods of my life, in connection with this subject, was the residence of a young woman in my house for a long period as a wet-nurse for our youngest child. She proved to be the best medium I ever met. This was nearly a score of years ago. She did not live long after her time was over with us. I hardly think I appreciated as I ought this remarkable privilege that I enjoyed. I had not the experience then that I have had since, but I have many times been led to appreciate the poetic truth, —

"That blessings brighten as they take their flight."

This young woman was a Catholic; did not know she was a medium. When I discovered the manifestations, she did not, in her ignorance, know what Spiritualism meant. She had almost every phase of the phenomena,— the movement of ponderable bodies without physical contact, raps on tables, chairs, and walls, at a distance or near; and, by her aid, all the old familiar names of departed friends, relations, and ancestors announced themselves, and often proved, in a remarkable manner, their identity. I often got the full names of people, and circumstances that I had to verify, proving her source of information to be both authentic, and beyond her knowledge and mine also until I had hunted up the matter.

We had not then reached in the history of Spiritualism the phase of materialization; I have no doubt she would have had that power also, if she had lived longer. She had the feature of materialization in its early type of that time, more apparent from the sense of touch than of sight. For instance: In a perfectly light room, perhaps of a sunny afternoon, seated around a small, square table, wife and I, *vis-a-vis*, this young woman on the side between us, sometimes a fourth person would occupy the other vacant side. but usually it was we three, our six hands were in sight flat on the table, then one of the hands being put under the table, leaving the other five hands before us in sight. The hand under the table could feel invisible hands, sensible to the touch, and intelligent in their manipulations. This was to us a new and very strange manifestation.

There was no deception about it, and could not be, under the circumstances. They improved and grew more distinct, even demonstrative, as we got interested in them. It was worthy of notice that some people who might make the fourth party were obstacles to the phenomenon. I certainly did not understand it, for it certainly was not due to any skeptical element in the new comer. Sometimes the party would be a Spiritualist who was the disturbing element, and by no means positive or mentally opposed, rather hoped for, and came expecting success, while sometimes the fourth party would not be a Spiritualist, had no faith in the belief, and we found no interruption with him to the manifestations.

This, certainly, shows that the obstacle is not a mental one, and, whatever it is, it seems to be constitutional,— a non-conducting element in the person. But I will not enlarge upon that point here; but, it being an unmistakable fact, it will show that the later and more extended phase of full-form materializations, the character of which good people differ, may be affected for better or worse by the persons constituting the circle.

I will close this chapter by describing some of my our experiences in this phase ; that is, where I put my hand under the table, of which I have spoken, and the remaining five hands being in sight on the table. I often had more than touches, or manipulations ; I very often grasped what seemed a human hand, and certainly was one, and certainly it was not the hand of a mortal in the form, nor a dummy. It was, apparently, flesh and blood and bones, and felt like anybody's or human hand.

These hands at different times were of different sizes and forms. Sometimes a child's hand, sometimes, by signification, it was a sister's hand, or a grandmother's. We all had this experience many times, I ought to say, myself, hundreds of times. My sister, who did much sewing when she was in the form, when the mysterious hand claimed to be hers, and tried to have me identify it, she allowed me to feel the end of her finger, the roughness of the cuticle that much sewing caused was perceptible and recognizable. I felt also the ring on her finger, and as far as touch without sight could tell, it seemed like her ring; but her ring then was owned by another party in another State, so it must have been evolved out of the circumambient air for the occasion, and the same, of course, of the hand itself, that is materialized.

One thing I will notice. No matter how firm a grip I might have had, I could never draw this spirit hand out into the light so that I could have ocular proof as well as proof by touch and manipulation. I would try sometimes to coax it out from under the table, and the hand seemed to make no objection, but it never would come; the grip would limber, the hand lose its density, and before it reached in my hand the end of the table for optical demonstration, I held nothing,— it had dissolved, so it never was an object of sight, though it was tangibly manifest.

I will have occasion to speak again of some experiences with this home-medium in other illustrations, so I will leave this matter here, having said sufficient for the purposes of this chapter, and certainly compensates for any leanness of thought in some of the inspired utterances referred to; for who will not say that the sensuous touch of a "vanished hand" externally, that is real in a material sense, is not more eloquent than words, and by the side of which the highest reaches of eloquence become insignificant and tame?

XI.

PRO–SPIRITUALISM.

An article written for, and published in, "The Radical."

When *The Radical*, a bright magazine, was alive, I was asked by its editor to write an article for it on modern Spiritualism. That showed the liberality of that able, "free religious" periodical, for the subject then was more in literary eclipse than it is now, though it is not yet out of the Philistinian domain.

As this article did not reach the eye of many Spiritualists, not being written for them, I have thought, though it was written nearly a decade ago, that I would copy it from that magazine for one of the chapters of this book. It is not exactly as I would have written it today, but much of it is worth perusal, and in some form should be herein presented, more, perhaps, for illustration of some of the other chapters of this book than for information. The following is the article to which I have referred : —

Modern Spiritualism addresses itself emphatically to the senses, differing fundamentally from all forms of religion in that respect, unless Roman Christianity be an exception. That, to be sure, addresses the senses, but only to the ignorant; the intelligent perceive significations underlying the symbols; but then the significations, becoming definite in such minds, are evangelical,—which means unscientific, hence anti-rational. So, I repeat, it differs from all other forms of religion on that point. Is it in conflict or in harmony with the inner sense or soul deep, which no mental plummet has ever yet sounded; which is marked on the oldest charts "no bottom;" and which, with all the additions of later or modern explorers, is still marked "no bottom?" Perhaps here is not the time or place to answer that question, only to think of it.

Of all ages, this is the inductive or practical age; and we are a people marked with inductive or practical tendencies. Dealing with facts is always popular, and has on its side the multitude, who observe rather than think, and, of course, are not inclined to listen to the more subtle teachings of the *prophets*, or those who live before their time,— that is, those who reason from intuitions or principles downward or outward to facts. Henry Thomas Buckle says: "Actions, facts, external manifestations of every kind, often triumph for awhile; but it is the progress of ideas which ultimately determines the progress of the world." I think few will dispute what is stated here on this point: and it reduces itself to this, viz., the observers are many, and the thinkers are few, and ultimately the thinkers rule the world.

Modern Spiritualism, its facts or phenomena, is

here, in triumph, "for awhile," if you choose. It may be here by virtue of the demand which the age has for facts, as a taste for dreams increases the crop of dreamers. It may be here to meet a want once supplied by faith,—that faith which science and reason (that is, rationalism) have killed. The logic of deduction from established principles, so called, is adverse to the claims of modern Spiritualism. The logic of induction has had no place in this connection. There have been heretofore no facts. The dead men *were* dead, and induction is inapplicable to and has no connection with theology; *that* is born of revelation, assumed. Therefore just as the logic of theology was adverse to the fact that the earth was a sphere, so is theology and all deductions from preconceived notions, however liberal in statement, adverse to the claim made by modern Spiritualism. The world demonstrated to be a sphere, there was revolution in the world of mind as well as in the world of matter. Demonstrate as clearly this fact, —or, rather, the claim based on the fact,—then behold another revolution. That point no one will dispute. But will it be demonstrated? What are the probabilities? The minds that reason from established principles (or notions true or false), or, to be more definite, a man who has the idea that heaven is more or less a church-gathering, where dignity and greatness have no light dressing of frivolity, but the redeemed " are as the angels in heaven," all human weaknesses having been left in the grave, and the free spirit, or the souls of men, all great, good, and perfect,—in a word, a sort of rationalized heaven with some or all the ancient evangelical features,— such will answer, and, as far as heard from, do, that the fact will *not* be demonstrated as a truth, and never ought to be: it would be a libel upon a sensible conception of heaven, the dwelling-place of the Infinite, and the resting-place for the weary pilgrims of earth.

I am aware I have no authority for reconstructing anyone's notion of heaven or its inhabitants, the abode either of the blessed or the disembodied; but, laying aside the "Planchette" authority, I have as much an anyone; and that, expressed by a symbol, is 0. That means, on this subject, assuming, for the moment, it is wholly devoid of fact, and wholly in the domain of faith, that the thinker or the philosopher has no right to assume what the facts or the phenomena ought to be from logical inferences, and, if antagonistic to his idea, reject on the ground of absurdity or triviality,—in other words, judge before a hearing. We came from monkeys says Charles Darwin. We may go back at death to first principles, or be monkeys again. No inference can possibly make us fear such a destiny; but no one can say it is not so; and, if investigations should demonstrate that fact, it is scientific to follow where the facts lead, and it is unscientific and irrational to reject phenomena, trivial or silly, which, existing, exist for some purpose, no matter what. We shall never know till we study it; and, in this connection, no matter the consequences to our hopes, our expectations or our vanity. "Where ignorance is bliss, 't is folly to be wise," may be evangelical : it is by no means rational.

I know of no subject so deserving of careful, tender, and critical attention as this one, whether in reference to its peculiar associations with our destiny or in reference to its wide-spreading influence as manifested in the multitude of its adherents. In a spirit of inquiry, then, not of dogmatism, let us look at the subject. I do so, hoping it to be true; but not prejudiced, I think, by that hope. From a great multitude of facts, let me select one, for a starting-point, from my own experience. I do not qualify the word : I mean fact. This detailed statement will be an episode in the argument, but it seems to be required as an aid or setting to the points I have in view. Here is the statement : —

Ellen was for many years a domestic in our family. Ann was a wet-nurse for our baby. Both were Irish and Catholics. Ellen was rather old, unmarried, steady, and faithful. Ann, the nurse, was a widow of about twenty,— ignorant, careless, and lively. There had been, in the month or two that they had lived together with us, several quarrels between them ; one quite serious, where it was necessary for me to interfere. Ann was accused by Ellen of pulling the kitchen table from her with her foot while kneading bread on it ; had done it, or similar pranks, many times. Ann said she did not, and Ellen said she did ; which led to a "rolling-pin" fight. And, without going into details too minutely, I had got to part with a healthy nurse or a faithful girl. A nurse, being a mother by proxy for the time, is mistress in the house. One cannot see his baby suffer. So we make sacrifices, "hang our harps upon the willows when we remember Zion," and pray for the weaning-time and freedom. Had it not been for her office, Ann would have been turned away without question, and at once. As it was, I conciliated Ellen, and compelled a truce.

In a short time, the same thing occurred up stairs. The light-stand seemed to be pulled away towards Ann. She was scolded by the mistress. Ann denied it, and in the plain evidence of the fact; for, while scolding, the table jumped. The secret was out: Ann was a medium. This girl did not know what "medium" signified; and had never heard of the word Spiritualism, and did not know its meaning or its associations. We visited the kitchen. The table moved a foot towards her, untouched. The whole matter was explained. There had been no lies told. As stated, we would have discharged, as a disturber and a liar, on positive evidence, and injured an innocent girl; in my ignorance, would have done an injustice. May not incarnated wisdom, higher up, be doing injustice now to some for their honest conclusions on this subject, that a more careful investigation might at least modify?

This matter was lengthily and critically examined under very favorable circumstances. The details are hardly needed here for my purpose. Ann's husband and father assumed to be the operators at the spirit end of the lines: and, through her, I got communi-

cations from many persons and relatives; often sometimes in reference to furniture and pictures they
once owned, given for tests, the details of which this
chance girl could know nothing of; many unknown
to myself, that inquiry proved to be true. After
going to confession, she refused to *sit* any more; said
her priest forbade it. He told her the spirit *was* her
father, etc.; but she must not sit any more. It was
wicked, and we were Protestants. The priest, then,
believed in the fact, it seemed.

The explanation of his objection did not seem to
be very intelligible or reasonable; but I make allow-
ances for the medium, in mundane matters, just as I
would one in spiritual. Persuasion overcame her
objections. I asked her if she still loved her father
and husband (who were still Catholics on the other
side). She did, and she believed with the priest,
that it was her father and her husband, as the communication claimed. "Then," said I, "suppose we
ask them?" If Ann had any inclination in the matter, it was that they would say: "Mind the priest."
Their reply was: "You do perfectly right to sit;
and we like it, too, and we love you."

As the details of this or any of the phenomena is
not the object of this communication, I will leave
what I have inserted here as an episode, and say that
this matter seems determined to be heard, and will
not down at anyone's bidding. The scientific jour-
nals, hitting the right point, say: "What is Planchette?" I do not expect science, as science, to
answer. Science deals with matter. When a great

question is asked seriously, in the course of time the interpreter will be born. He is as likely to be a carpenter's son as a Gamaliel; rather more so, if any conclusions for the future can be gathered from past experience: the author of "Ecce Homo" says the world is grandly debtor to lowly cradles, which is a truth.

An anti-Spiritualist, in the *Atlantic Monthly*, has been in the front, and seen the phenomena. Now, there is something in it, it has come to me, says he. Professors explain it. They still neglect the unclean thing, saying to this writer: "Watch it carefully: you are deceived." He is snubbed; *he*, who is religious and respectable, not one of those Spiritualists. He forgets it is not the man that makes the matter worthy of notice: it is the matter that degrades the man, as yet. This late writer tells his story outside of the ring of fools. No more a fact for that; but it shows extension, pressing for expression on the line of least resistance. It has got beyond the deluded; and, as the volume expands, the fracture extends through this late and tougher material. If this subject is mythical, we shall know it in the next age if not in this. In the meantime, let us soberly treat it. Spiritualism is the only form of religion that America has yet produced; (please not suggest Mormonism in this connection, — that *de facto* is not confined to Utah or America); and, aside from its super-mundane claims, is, as to its ethics, just what a free people, who, in flowering out, produced the Declaration of Independence, might suppose to develop as a religion. It is essentially *independence, liberty,* and *progress*, in perfect harmony with the last circle of the Protestant wave,— Parkerism, or free religion; just what *The Radical* represents all but the one fact, that disembodied Theodore Parker not only lives, but speaks to and through mortals. . . . . ..

Humanity grows; and in this age of facts, when everything is met and handled in the inductive or analytic spirit, which is the logical condition of human progress, I am led to ask what the heart-tendrils will reach hold of and entwine to support this human vine? I have the many in my mind, not the richly endowed few, wealth of thought. Can anyone believe that God has left us without a witness, not of himself, that evidence is everywhere, but of his justice? It is nowhere in material philosophy. I go, says Faith; but I will send the Comforter, and it will teach you all things. It must needs be that I, Faith, go. If I go not, the Comforter will not come. In the midst of rationalism, I am looking for what it has not in itself,— the Comforter. Has God left us without the witness? Mr. Weiss has it. He feels *his* immortality. That satisfies him: he needs no tables to tip for him. He gave Theodore Parker the witness. He was sure of the *other* world: this was the one he doubted. But why give to Weiss and Frothingham and Parker and Bartol, and not the many like this writer? Must the many take it on trust? Because a few prophets have the evidence, must the rest have only faith? Rationalism says: No authority but *truth*. Whose truth? Why not Calvin's as well as Parker's?

Will God take away, by the law of progress, almost universal faith, and leave me without a ray of hope? Because Weiss & Co. are fed with their own deductions, and thrive by it, must I starve? Because Weiss's clover will not feed me, must I fall back on worms? In the midst of his satisfying clover, must Elijah starve because there are no ravens?

It would seem as though the only witness that the age demands, or can satisfy it, is a voice from the tomb. Here are phenomena that answer that demand in its claims. True, it may be an hallucination. For reasons already mentioned,— its increasing influence, and its moral effect,— is not its particular fact worthy of attention? Is there any reason why, in writing in its defense, I should lose something of my moral and intellectual position, unless I weave into the structure of my communication the *respectable* fact or apology that the writer is not a believer in the spiritual explanation of these phenomena? He makes in this instance no such excuse.

Now, here is the fact desired,— *if it be a fact.* If it be the once dead speaking, has there been so important a question ever considered? Shall we reject it because it keeps company with Publicans and sinners? Shall we refuse to wash and be clean because the river is simply Jordan? Shall we say: "What manner of departed spirits are these that play on fiddles, and dance tables; that rap loud and soft on tables, walls, and doors?" Shall we say: "Nonsense!" while they every time say: "I am one of

thy brethren, the prophets"? Why, it violates all my
ideas of respect for the departed, and their condition.
"How are the mighty fallen!" Shades of great
Franklin! you are in twenty places at the same
time, and all unknown to each other. He must be a
double-header. Oh, no! foolish dream!—I had
rather be without the proof, the sweet evidence of
life beyond the vale, if such is to be the end of all
my greatness.

In this connection, bear in mind, there have been
more atheists and infidels converted from their materialism to a belief in the soul's continued existence
than by all the religious and rational logic during
the same time. The great number, among whom is
this writer, who have by these puerile phenomena,
perceiving the underlying truth irrespective of its
details and associations, who have passed from darkness to light and hope, is a fact or a good so important as should command a tender regard for it, set as
it is so poorly. Pebbles become jewels sometimes by
their setting. Here may be a jewel spoiled by its
setting. Common sense (which is vulgar for rationalism) says: "Prove it worthless, or reset it."

It may be stated here, and truly, that Spiritualists
do not claim for it admission as a demonstrated truth,
to be universally accepted, unchallenged. They, of
all people, say: "Examine for yourselves, and believe
or reject as your conviction dictates." There may
be, and probably is, more error than truth in it.
What venerated institution but must make the same
confession? Who would except the church on this

point? Speaking for myself, the communication of disembodied spirits with mortals *is* a demonstrated truth. I make this statement with some little critical knowledge of mental phenomena, or what is called the psychical side of life. A less cautious person, on the same evidence, might also speak equally strong of *identity*. The identity of individual spirits is by no means so established, even in a Spiritualist's mind, as that more indefinite one of disembodied intelligence. In a word (I am speaking for no one but myself now), there is no positive proof that Theodore Parker ever spoke to or through a mortal. The chances favor the assumption that he may have done so, even if the result be silly,—de-Parkerized by the process. But that a disembodied spirit, claiming to be Theodore Parker, or was once some special dweller of earth, has communicated through mortals, is to me no more a matter of doubt than that a man lives in Europe claiming to be Victor Hugo. The identity of the living is easy of demonstration; of the other, not so easy.

The obstacle is not in the quality of thought offered as Theodore Parker's. We do not know how spirit or mind controls matter, only that, under certain conditions, it does; and we know, further, that matter controls spirit also; that intemperance in eating may produce a condition of body, or rather of mind, incapacitating it for its master-pieces; and Homer nods, or becomes Homer and water, even in the form, *before* he goes to the spirit life. But we would assume, or some would, that we know all the conditions of transit and association, between spirit and mortal life, when we know comparatively nothing of the connection between our own souls and bodies. Shall we say, then, there is nothing practical in it?—all unreliable? Let it be so. That is another part of the subject. No thoughtful person will reject the fundamental fact, if he knows it to be a fact, because all we expected or hoped for is not available. Perhaps as yet there is not enough of the curve given us to measure the circle; and in time we may be qualified.

With all the crudities in connection with this subject, I venture the prophecy that this fact, being fundamentally a truth, has come to stay; and that this generation shall not pass away before the church as a general thing will adopt it, and it will be the warm blood that will give it life. Thus not only will it be a feature, but it will be claimed as always having been a feature,— latent for awhile, having been mixed up with superstition; but the old remembrances will be heated red-hot again, and the image and superscription be made in its reproduction to bear testimony not only to the fact, but to its antiquity also. And thus again a stone which the builders rejected will have become the head of the corner.

XII.

HOME MANIFESTATIONS.

Giving a brief account of phenomena which are both "bottom facts" and "startling facts."

I had been a Spiritualist four or five years when the opportunity opened to me of which I have spoken in a previous chapter. It seems to me now that the circumstance was a providential one (using the word, not in any divine sense, but only in a modern spiritual one, which is all the providence I know anything about), that this young woman should have proved a sort of "gates ajar" to me.

The article from *The Radical*, in the last chapter, refers to her in an illustrative way, but I think I had better briefly speak of her again, having some circumstances to relate in connection with her that are of marked importance, if there be any importance in argument or experiences.

When there had been trouble in the kitchen between Ann (the name of the nurse) and the domestic, it was presumed there had been mischief and lying of some kind, but the nurse held the fort, as a matter of course, for the life and health of the baby were in her hands. A week or two after this affair, the table in the sitting-room, at which my wife and Ann were sitting and sewing, showed a disposition to be self-active. It actually jumped and almost upset the lamp that was on it, and would had there not been intelligence in the movement.

My wife said to Ann : "Be careful and not hit the table, you will set us on fire." "I did not do it," said she, and the table jumped again,—markedly so, —and both looked at each other. "Did you not do that?" wife said; and Ann replied: "No, marm, I did not." Wife felt uneasy, and called up Ellen from the kitchen, who was told what had happened; and the table, as if hearing them talk, began its antics again, no one touching it. Ellen saying to it: "Stop!" but it jumped the more, and all three women were surprised and frightened. Ellen then said, looking at it firmly: "In Christ's name, stop!" —making the sign of a cross with her finger, and it stopped, and no further movement was noticed.

This was in the evening. When I got home, which was soon after, I was told the circumstances, and I said to Ann that she must be a medium, and asked her to sit down with me at the table; and then, lay- ing our hands on it, I said, if there were any spirits present let us know it in some way; and, in response, in a few seconds there was a mild movement, also raps; and, asking who it was, and using the alpha- bet, the name of a relative was spelled out; and as soon as I recognized and mentioned the name, the table signified its satisfaction with applause, if moving rapidly may be called applause.

I will not inflict upon the reader any lengthy details of what this beginning led to, but will say I had in my two years' experience all the evidence that anyone could desire, that this table, or the invisibles manifesting through it, knew a great deal that this girl could not have known, and many things of a traditional character from some of my departed friends that I had myself to verify. The point to mention now is about that row, of which I have spoken, which occurred in the kitchen a short time before.

We then went into the kitchen. Ann took her place at the end of the table, where she was at the time spoken of. Ellen, the other girl, stood in front of it, resting her hands on it as if the bread-board was before her; and I said: "I wish, if there are any spirits here, they would move the table;" and it startled us by its jumping a foot. The whole matter explained itself. Ann did not shove the table at the time referred to. So, when she said to Ellen: "She did n't," she did not lie, as Ellen thought she did. The rumpus was explained, and the discovery and the succeeding conveniences of protracted manifestations are among the most interesting circumstances in my life, as I have already said.

I understand the matter now better than I did then. This occurred during my first decade in my connection with Spiritualism. I am now near the end of my third decade. It is possible my remarkable opportunities have saved me in the line so as to see a third decade. When these home manifestations came to me it lowered my estimation of the spirit world in dignity. Why did it want to disturb my kitchen affairs? I learned later that it was to attract attention. I am very glad, then, it so stooped for my benefit, but I cannot even yet think I was of consequence enough for it, or any part of it. It certainly has added to my happiness, if not to my reputation, to have a knowledge of this subject, and be interested in it. I hope the spirit world is not sorry it thus waked me up, or wasted thought or time on me ; but if a man is only a bramble-bush, he cannot bear grapes or figs.

In speaking on this point, it reminds me how much I have had to combat with people's sense of propriety. "It cannot be spirits," say they; "have they nothing better to do than to tip tables and play poorly on musical instruments, with the lights out?" "Seems to me," say some, "if I were a spirit, I would hope to be better employed; I would not do such things now, and I hope I shall not lower myself when I have done with earth and become an angel." People are inclined to look at the act itself, not what prompts the act, and there is where such people are wrong.

I look at these things now very differently from what I once did. There is no fascination, instruction, or entertainment in the movement of material things in the way mentioned, simply as movements ; but if one is persuaded that it is a departed spirit,

taking that way to make you realize his or her presence, is there then not fascination,— not in the thing,
or the grotesque movement, but in the invisible intelligence that is manifesting through or with it?

Now, with these considerations, notice the following incident in my experience. I state it as a positive fact, as unmistakable a one as the fact that I am
now writing these words. I will do it elaborately,
for it made a deep impression upon me, so have also
many others, but I will relate this one as an illustration of my point.

I was sitting at the window, in our sitting-room,
reading a newspaper one afternoon. My wife was
resting on a sofa on the other side of the room. In
the center of it, and not very far from me, was a
small table. Ann — this Endoric member of my
household — was sitting, not at, but very near, this
table, sewing, or repairing some dress, and at the
table was a little son of mine, some six or seven years
old. Hearing some raps on the table, he said: "Is
that you, Hattie?" (that was the name of his sister
who had died some years before) and the response to
his question was three raps. We all heard them,
which meant, in spiritual parlance: "Yes." The
little fellow then says: "Oh, mother, Hattie is here,
she says so!" "Well," says the mother, "go on and
talk with her, and see what she will say."

The boy then said: "Hattie, have I been a good
boy today?" and the answer was three raps, or
"yes." And while asking one or two questions in
this way, the supper-bell rang, and the little boy,

while getting off the stool on which he was sitting, said : "Hattie, will you come and talk to me after tea?" And the mother, as she arose from the sofa, said : "Why do n't you ask her to come down to supper with you?" We were amused to see him take her literally, as he said: " Hattie, will you come down to supper with me?" And as he said this, he had got off of his stool, and the table, untouched, was tipping in reply; and as the little fellow moved then towards the door, the table followed him, nobody touching it,—it seemed to slide along smoothly towards the door. When it got to the threshhold, which was a little obstruction, it paused a second, and then jumped over the slight elevation, and continued its movement a few feet to the head of the stairs, seemed to make an effort or two as if tipping, then stopped.

Now, as I have said, I am stating literally the exact truth. It being so, was not that an intelligent act? Did not the invisible intelligence controlling that table hear the little boy's question, and could he, she, or it say any plainer than this movement: "Yes, I thank you, I will go with you." The poet tells us there are sermons in stones. I believe it ; and sometimes these voiceless orations are more eloquent than are the uttered words of a master. It does seem to me as if the bright words of the most eloquent preacher pale and sink into insignificance by the side of such mute preaching as the movement of that table, showing the interest of a departed sister in her little brother in the form.

I hardly know how to stop, so many of these experiences crowd into my mind, as if pressing for expression; but I will hold them back, and close this chapter by relating a circumstance of a different kind, but certainly of a very convincing and encouraging character.

On one occasion, when Ann had been sitting for us, and with us for over a year, she declined to sit; said she was not going to do so any more. Being pressed for the reason, she said the priest had told her she must not. Ann was a Catholic, but had not been to confession since she came to live with us, but she had lately been, and, among her other sins, confessed to sitting with us for these manifestations. She wanted to oblige us, but was afraid to.

This priest had told her that the spirits who came were really the spirits of Andrew and Peter (the names of her husband and father), but that she did not belong to that or our circle. That sitting with us for such a purpose was wicked, and forbid it in the usual Catholic way. I tried to persuade her, but did not succeed, so I became strategetic, and said to her: "You say the priest said the spirits that came were your husband and father?" "Yes," said she, "the priest said so." "Were they good Catholics?" "Yes," said she. "And you thought a good deal of them, did you?" "Oh, certainly!" "Which do you think would know better what was right, your husband and father, who are now spirits in the other world, or the priest, who has not been there yet?" She hesitated, but said she thought they would.

"Now," says I, "Ann, I do not want you to do anything wrong, but I want you to sit just once, to ask Andrew and Peter whether it is right or wrong, for they will know,— will they not? and the priest says they are really Andrew and Peter." She could not object to so reasonable a request, and she did so; and, the raps coming, says I: "Who is this?" And the reply was: "Andrew." Says I: "Andrew, is it wrong for Ann to sit in this way for these manifestations?" And the reply was a loud "No." "Do you think Ann had better sit for us, as she has been doing?" And the answer came: "Yes." "You see," said I to Ann, "what your father and husband both say, and you know it is really they, for the priest says it is, and they, being in the spirit world, ought to know better than the priest, had they not?" And Ann thought so, and made no further objection.

The remembrance of this colloquy, growing out of her confession, always pleased me; I flanked the priest adroitly from his own logic. I also got the admission, indirectly, of him that the manifestations were the work of spirits. It was always pleasant also to have Ann feel that her father and her husband had a hand in this matter. I ought to add, which may be suggestive, also, that Andrew and Peter were the spirits that did most of this mysterious work, that is, when a table moved, they were the spirits that did it, or they seemed to be the spirits that controlled her, certainly for the sensuous or physical manifestations.

I have found in many instances that the spirits

who make these physical manifestations, or movements, are not the higher class of spirits, but spirits
who are but a slight remove from palpable presence.
I have been told that Theodore Parker cannot move
a material object, or tip a table, but he can read the
mind and influence the intellect; that it is a more
earthly class of spirits that, in this sensuous way,
make themselves manifest. My experience with Ann
seems to rather indorse the idea.

XIII.

SEERSHIP OR CLAIRVOYANCE.

*Giving an account of phenomena with an intelligent
and sometimes a prophetic basis.*

> "And that should teach us
> There 's a divinity that shapes our ends,
> Rough-hew them how we will."— *Shakespeare.*

If, when Henry W. Longfellow, in his poetical
address to his class in Bowdoin College, on its fiftieth
anniversary, said : —

> "Not to the living only be they said,
> But to that other living, called the dead,"

it was not a fancy merely, but a truth ; that if he
really felt or believed that there was an unseen audience as well as a visible one listening to him,— or, to
express the thought in another way, if there is a spiritual environment around this world of sense,— then
the divinity referred to that doth hedge us about, as
the poet says, is a very rational idea. I think a better
word than "divinity" could be used to express it,
but the fact would be all the same ; and you know a
rose by any other name would smell as sweet.

This fact of such an environment being admitted, how it seems to warm up this world, illuminating the whole picture of human life. Everything then puts on new forms of beauty, changing deformity and fable into beauty and truth. I do not propose now to argue this point, and make such an environment appear either reasonable or truthful. It is a fact to me, and I merely say what I have stated as a sort of setting to an interesting fact in my family experience, which, in connection with this subject, is worth relating.

There are many similar cases; in fact, traditional as well as general family records are full of legendary lore, mysterious or superstitious, or otherwise, out of repute as good common sense, that the fact being demonstrated of a spiritual world surrounding and permeating this, would come into line as both possible and respectable facts. That is the reason why the one I propose to relate, under the light of my spiritualistic ideas, will, I think, be a matter of interest.

My grandmother was a seeress. I lived in the house with her for the first twenty years of my life, and for ten or fifteen years more, near by, supervising her until she died. Now, while her spirit which now seems to be in my surroundings, and also the spirit of her daughter, my mother, I feel moved to use the words of Coleridge (in his "Sibylline" lines, I think) as my own : —

> "Blest spirits of my parents,
> Ye hover o'er me now! Ye shine on me!

And, like a flower that coils forth from a ruin,
I feel and seek the light I cannot see."

What would I not give to have the advantage today that I had during her lifetime. But I was like the disciples at Emmaus, who did not realize the departed Master's presence until he had gone. With the optics of today, or my spiritualistic experience to notice the phenomena of which I am going to speak, that occurred from 1825 to 1845, that would, indeed, be a privilege.

This ancestor was a good and sensible woman, rather sickly, or thought she was, being of a nervous constitution. The household, consisting of her sons and daughters and a few grandchildren, knew nothing of seeresses or seers in their day, but considered her clairvoyant sights as simply imagination or nervousness. Certainly, her best clairvoyant visions were when she was not feeling well, or under the weather, as we sometimes say. We all considered what she saw, and which nobody else saw in this way, was the product of poor health, and had no foundation really, though they seemed real to her. We pitied her, but loved and respected her, as otherwise she was a very gifted woman, with sterling, human, motherly qualities, but hurt some by this mixture of the mysterious and strange, or of a superstitious character.

All her life, or all I know of it, which was her last thirty years, she could see the spirits of dead people, as she called them, though they always looked alive, or as they did when they were alive. Hardly a week passed without her referring to such visits. They were, as I have said, more persistent or frequent when her health was poor; hence, in the minds of the family, the subject was looked upon as disease.

These subjective apparitions were always the forms and faces of departed people, never of living ones,— generally relatives, brothers, sisters, or her children. She was one of a family of twelve, and she was the mother, also, of twelve, and my mother was the last of them to pass away a few years ago, aged eighty-four. Most of her children had died in young manhood or womanhood, so there were many to come to her in this way, and they very often did. I think everyone of her brothers and sisters, my great uncles and aunts, had at one time or another put in their ghostly appearance, if such phenomena can be called appearances. I am as familiar with them, from her description when thus appearing, as I am traditionally, as the greater part of them died before I saw them.

Notwithstanding the family-feeling that these "second-sights," as they were called, were weaknesses that better health or a less nervous or sensitive organization would have relieved her from, none of us liked to have her tell of any ominous ones that might be premonitions,—"showing," as Dr. Johnson said, "by our fears our faith in them," for they were very apt to be previsions. I will relate one that I remember well, as it made a great impression on me, and this will suggest the character of some of the others.

On one occasion this old lady said to me that she felt very down-hearted,—that she had had a vision that made her feel so. Her dead children had not come as they generally did, as if they were alive and happy; but they had come in such a way as to make her feel as if she was going to have a grief. She said she saw two of her dead children, George and Edward, and both came to her in coffins, standing against the wall, with their lids hanging down, exposing their dead faces.

They did not look happy and natural, as these specters usually did, but represented themselves as corpses,—eyes closed, motionless, and dead. That was not all: for there were three coffins in a row,—George in one, Edward in the other; and then Barney was in a coffin, too, his standing in the middle; "and Barney is alive, and I am afraid," said she, "that something is going to happen." She evidently felt that Barney, who was then living in New Orleans, was going to die. This was forty years ago before there was any railroad there, and no telegraph.

How distinctly I remember the following incident, about two weeks after the date of this vision of the three coffins. We were all sitting in the parlor of our two-story house, in Roxbury, when we heard the garden-gate open, and she said: "Oh! it is a letter coming, and I do n't want to see it." And she went up stairs. In a second or two the door-bell was rung, and a letter left by the post-boy, with a black seal on it. It was written by a friend of Barney's, informing us of his sudden sickness and death.

It seems to me the symbol of the coffins, as I have described them, was a very intelligent and expressive one. Could any communication be more expressive of the fact than this was,— the open coffins of three of her children, showing three dead faces? Could there be any mistake in what was meant or intended? If a voice had said, or if George and Edward had said, "Barney has just died," would the fact have been more distinctly or intelligently conveyed than was this mute way of symbolizing the fact?

Is there any royal road or occult way of getting information? Here was an occurrence twelve days before it was possible, in that day, to have been known by us. Everybody is liable to die, but Barney no more than anybody else. He was not sick, and only about thirty-five or forty years old. I am aware there are sometimes premonitions; so there are dreams sometimes that have an intelligent method in them, that in some inscrutable way are pre-visions of coming events, casting, as it were, their shadows before.

If there are divinities shaping human ends, which in most peoples' minds is simply a poetic fancy; but if it be a reality, as modern Spiritualism teaches,— that we live in two worlds, but cognizant of but one,— then this vision, which I have related at length, becomes an intelligent act on the part of the angel world. Can it be anything else?

I like the closing words of an able agnostic minister of a discourse on immortality, which are these: "Though I do find this life sweet, I do want another;

and though I cannot go as far as some and say this
life is not worth having if there be no other, I do
say dust and ashes seem a somewhat poor and impo-
tent conclusion for such a magnificent, grand, terri-
ble life drama as that we are playing here on this old
earth,—

> ' I cannot think it all shall end in naught;
> That the abyss shall be the grave of thought.
> That e'er oblivion's shoreless sea shall roll
> O'er love and wonder and the lifeless soul.' "

XIV.

SUBJECTIVE APPARITIONS.

A visit of consolation where the consoler got consoled.

There seems to be a power in the soul or spirit of man which at times projects itself, or its visible personality, and shows itself at a great distance, and, it would seem instantly, no matter whether the distance be one mile or ten thousand miles. This most generally occurs just at the point of death. Instances of this fact are numerous. Most of these appearances, as I have said, occur just at the moment of death, as if that event was the fulcrum necessary to produce it; but instances are not rare when these appearances have occurred at other periods in a person's life.

These subjective forms look exactly as the person did,— a natural, human-appearing person, leading the seer to think, or say: "How did he get here when I supposed he was so far off?" and then to find it only a seeming or a fancy, when, sooner or later, we hear of the person's death, and it generally proves to have been at the moment of the appearing. It would seem to be a sort of soul appearing to soul, and shows by the manifestation that there is a spiritual man as well as a physical man that can exist separately, or the fact of a man's spirit existing distinct from his body.

I do not think it argues against this deduction by saying it occurs only at the moment of death, which is not the fact, as I have said. I could state an instance in my own experience if it were worth the while to do so. To me, the appearance of the person at death seems to be as if intelligently informing the beholder of his final departure.

I was well acquainted with our late citizen, Col. Wm. B. Green, the author of the "Blazing Star," well known among us as a theoretical labor-reformer and philanthropist during the last few years of his life. I saw him quite often; he was not a Spiritualist, but was very hospitable to the idea. His daughter, a fair-haired maiden of about twenty, was drowned off the coast of France, being one of the passengers of a steamer that was there lost. She had left this country a few weeks before. I think this was on her voyage out, but it may not have been, as I am writing from memory.

When the news came of the loss of the steamer, and of her loss, I took an early opportunity of calling upon Col. Green from sympathy and respect, and found him much better prepared to meet his grief than I expected, which was explained when he told me he had the announcement of her departure from earth a few days or a week before, though hoping otherwise, that the information in advance of earthly information was an illusion. When the news was cabled of the loss of the steamer, and she among the lost, he then felt it was all right, for he had seen her since the event, and he related to me the following circumstance : —

In the night he awoke, or was awake, and saw, to his surprise and wonder, his daughter. She was clothed in white, as if wearing a wedding-garment (it was his expression), with a bright smile of happiness on her face, and pointing upwards. She disappeared, apparently, out of the room into the next chamber, where his wife, her mother, was sleeping, and she, it seemed, saw the same vision,— that is, the daughter was seen by both father and mother. Col. Green said it was no dream, for he was wide awake. This call, on my part, was intended to be one of a consoling character. I knew the loss he had met with, and expected, or at least hoped, to have given him, from some of my experience in *post-mortem* matters, some consolation. I knew that he respected me, and knew of my belief, for we had talked together on the subject, and that anything I said would be both honest and from my heart.

As I said, he needed no consolation. He was happy, felt that it was all right, and he looked as rationally on her departure from earth as he did when she left home on her philanthropic mission to Europe (it was some charitable undertaking that she became interested in, I think, of a Catholic character). Mr. Green's glowing account of this interesting circumstance made him my consoler instead of my consoling him.

This is not my experience, but the experience of my friend, as he related it to me, and I know he was truthful; so I tell the story. With my experience in these things, I remember how I was lifted up both in my knowledge and faith by the joy he manifested at having such an angelic visit.

I will now relate a circumstance of a cognate character from my own experience. This was many years ago, but it made a vivid impression on me at the time, and has never been forgotten. I relate the circumstance not so much for itself as for its connection with later events, down even to the present time.

My mother had a favorite sister, Emeline; she was my aunt, and was one of the most loveable young women that ever lived. We, myself and two sisters, loved her like a mother, and she loved and cared for us. In early womanhood, she gradually went into a decline with consumption, and, after failing away for many months, she passed to the higher life. Of course, with that disease, death was expected. It was only a question of time; it might be months, and it might be a year or two. She had changed from a rosy-cheek young woman to a pale and emaciated one, but her interest in us, and her loveableness, were permanent and enduring.

One evening, seated by the table, mother busy sewing, and I getting my school-lesson; my two sisters, near the same age, and a year or two younger than I was, were asleep in the curtained bed at the other end of the room. Sarah, the older of the two, and the special favorite of Emeline, suddenly screeched out as if in distress, and mother ran to the bedside to see what was the matter. Sarah, agitated and frightened, said: "Aunt Emeline just pulled aside the curtain and looked right at me, and she smiled and nodded as she did so; she looked so lean and death-like that I am frightened." "Oh," said mother, "go right to sleep, you were only dreaming; nobody has been into the room. John and I have been sitting here all the time, and poor, sick Emeline has not been off her bed for a month" (she was occupying the chamber under ours). "No, mother," said Sarah, "I was not asleep, had not been asleep, and had heard you and John talking, so it was really Emeline her own self, for I saw her; do n't I know aunt Emeline? I saw her with my eyes just as plainly as I am now seeing you, and she looked right into my face." As Sarah said this, our grandmother came into the room, weeping, and said: "Emeline has gone; she has just died."

This appearance was a reality to Sarah, and from the circumstance of just having died, or had left her body lying on the bed in the room, it was an intelligent notice, by her appearance to her little pet, that she had died, and had stopped a minute in her departure to say, in that mute way, good-bye. She thought everything of her little Sarah; they were as much attached as if they were mother and child.

I have sometimes wondered why this spirit, for it must have been a spirit (as her body had not moved)

should appear so lean and pale and deathly, the picture of her bodily form, for the spirit had not died,
or had a consumption; but, then, if she did not
appear as she was then known, she might not have
been recognized. I prefer, however, to think, and have
good reason to, as these "Shadows" in their wholeness will show, that spirits in the "land of light and
beauty" are free from their physical imperfections
and disabilities, and so to leave such an impression,
as it rests in my own mind, I will add the following
fancy verse: —

> "A ghost! by my cavern it darted!
>   In moonbeams the spirit was drest, —
> For lovely appear the departed
>   When they visit the dreams of my rest!"

XV.

EMELINE'S APPARITION.

Other "white ladies" besides the one of Avenel, related by Sir Walter Scott.

Emeline, of whom I have spoken in the preceding chapter, died over fifty years ago, when my two sisters and I were children. Since I have been a Spiritualist, which dates from the year 1857, I have had many proofs of her continued existence, and her interest in my family or tribe, so to speak. I have sometimes thought of her as the "white lady," referring to "The white lady of Avenel," in Sir Walter Scott's novel of the "Monastery."

I cannot say her influence or presence has been significant of trouble or death, as the novelist's "white lady" was; yet it has often been so, and a very vivid impression of her presence would make me a little uneasy now, and yet she has, more than once, shown an interest and a marked supervision for our good, and so remarkable that I count them, or at least one of them among my best experiences; yet, as I have said, when I feel certain of her contiguity, I am apt to think that something is going to happen our family or tribal interest. (160)

On a certain Monday evening not very long ago (it was in the spring of 1883, I see by an article of mine, which is now in print before me), I seated myself at the writing table in my library for a few hours' work that I had been putting off, and then I felt that it must be attended to. A restless feeling came over me, and the image of Aunt Emeline came strangely into my mind. Such accidental images or thoughts are of no special importance, unless they are persistent and will not depart at the wishing. When an image or presence of a spirit "sticks," using Charles Sumner's expressive word, I have learned to consider it an indication of such a spirit, and, of course, for a purpose; but for what purpose? There is the rub.

I hardly feel like enlarging on this point. The reader, I trust, will conclude from the character of these "Shadows" that I think I know what I am talking about; if not, as I have said before, he or she must skip me. "Barkis is willin'."

My sister's husband, Albert——, a very dear friend of mine, and one of the best men that ever lived, came into my mind with this imaginary presence of Aunt Emeline. I know of no reason why they should have been thus associated, only I state the fact, and their persistency in my mind disturbed me in my work, and I gave it up. I found the conditions were not right, and yet, as many know, I am one who can make his own conditions. When I found that these thoughts of Emeline and Albert were "holding the fort," and the work I was doing was not, I gave up to it and cogitated. It would be tedious to write the details and explain the adroitness of circumstances and coincidences that mixed the two names together, — the image of the spirit and the image of the mortal, — so I will not attempt it. I have been a student or close observer of these "phantoms of the brain" for a long while, and I know I am not deluded in my conclusions of the fact; the purpose is what bothers me.

Albert was a man in poor health, and had been for years. For many years he had great pain in his head from a diseased ear; and having, myself, a catarrh, which might be of a similar character, and that also of long standing but no pain, seemed to be a pointer to the circumstance. Albert had been urging me for a long time to attend to it so as not to suffer as he had, but I had not felt the necessity of it. I could see no other unit of measure to explain this mental association of the two but this common auricular trouble. I began to consider it a gentle warning, and mentally concluded at an early moment to attend to it. The presence, if it were one, and the associations having thus monopolized my time, the evening's work was postponed. I was not in the mood to attend to it or anything else, owing to these unexpected and weird thoughts.

The next morning (Tuesday) among my letters I found one from my sister in Rhode Island, dated the day before, saying Albert, her husband, had just died. It took me by surprise, for I knew that he was out attending to business a day or two before. This explained the presence of this " white lady" and her

connection with Albert, which I had associated with
a common ear trouble, but it seems to me it was a
"phantomatic whisper," the best it could do to impress
me of my friend's death and, perhaps, presence also.

On my way home that afternoon I stopped at a
spiritual meeting a few minutes. A medium on the
platform was giving tests to the audience. They
generally do not amount to much, are given, it seems
to me, as an advertisement, so I was not interested
in them, and was reading a newspaper instead; but as
I sat thus at the end of the hall, this medium said:
"I hear the name of Albert,—yes, Albert is here.
He seems to be attracted here by some friend of his."
I felt from the first that it was my Albert, who had
so lately died, and the name was for me, but I said
nothing.

The medium then said: "It is for some one in that
direction," pointing towards me. I said: "Has he
been in the spirit world some time?" "No," said
the controlling spirit, "he has just come over. It is
for you, sir," addressing me, "he seems glad that you
recognize him. He says, 'John, I begin to understand these things better than I did. You know I
did not believe as much as you did, but I see it now
as you do.'" Then the control continuing, said,
"John, I have no pain now, no pains in my head;
none of those noises that I used to tell you of." This
was substantially what he said, and I wrote it down
at the time. It certainly was remarkably applicable.

It was a simple name,—Albert; that might have
been a guess, but when was added the exact views

he had of Spiritualism, it made two good guesses, and then he spoke of his head and pain and noises, of which he and I had had many talks in life. This takes the matter wholly out of guess-work and satisfies me, and would anyone with like experience, that it was my friend Albert, and that the Monday night "phantoms of the brain" were real presences also. I was wholly unacquainted with this medium, still I may have been known to him, probably was. I am sure nobody there knew that I had lost an Albert, and I do not think anyone knew that I had such a relative, as he had never been among the Spiritualists, and lived in another State.

I will now relate an experience which shows an actual supervision by a spirit over a mortal in the form.

Sometimes spiritual supervision is so definite as to be unmistakable of itself, so self-evidently true that it cannot be coincidence or imagination; its definiteness forbids it. Such visits certainly are like the fabled angels' visits, few and far between. The only drawback to such a case being a literal fact in anyone's mind is their unfrequency, and perhaps the special matter not always being of importance enough to call for angelic supervision.

If the importance is the factor in such cases, then life is full of demands that call for aid and supervision in vain, so there must be exoteric conditions of which we know nothing, or the supervising definition of what is considered of importance is different from ours. Here is an experience of a supervising intelligence, which is quite remarkable, and from the nature of the case could not have been accidental. It will be an interesting account in itself, as well as an illustration to the principal feature or point in this chapter.

My sister's daughter, or niece of mine, whom in this sketch I will call Mary, was making us a visit. She was a young lady of about sixteen, very interesting and well educated. From something I had said, she spoke of some "spiritual manifestations," and on what had occurred at her school on a certain occasion, which made me say: "Mary, you must be a medium." "No, I guess not, uncle," she said, as if the appellation was not complimentary, she not having had any experience with Spiritualists or Spiritualism, and had the usual social prejudices.

I said to her: "Come and sit at the table with me." She did so; but there being no raps or tipping, after a little while I said to her: "Hold this pencil in your hand," offering her one, and laying some sheets of paper on the table, she holding the pencil as if she was going to write. Her hand was still for a little while, then began a slight motion, which grew very rapid, so that the pencil end made a lot of dots, but no writing. "Is not this strange, uncle?" said she; "see how my hand jumps; I cannot help it; I do not do it; it does it itself;" which was very evident.

After a little while the pencil began to write, and very rapidly filled the page, which I took up, and she, without stopping, began to fill another, and so on, filling four pages, signing the last one "Emeline Clap." I was very much interested both in the fact and the contents, as I read the communications as she wrote them, as I took up the sheets one after another. The young lady knew nothing of the contents of the communication, as the reader will hereafter see from the nature of it; and she kept saying while she was writing: "Is not this strange, uncle, that my hand is writing so, and I do n't do it?" When she had finished, the pencil flew out of her hands with a jerk, and I said to her: "Do you know who Emeline Clap is?" "No," said she; "but do n't you know, as the name is Clap?" (our ancestral name). I said to her very impressively, as I was rather astonished at the contents: "She is your mother's and my aunt, who died long before you were born, and when your mother was a little girl. Holding the sheets in my hand, I then read the message aloud. Here is a copy: —

"My dear Mary, I have come to warn you, and to give you good advice. The course you are pursuing is wrong. You are having you think a pleasant time; but you are doing yourself an injury, and are injuring Mr. Chick. He is nothing to you, and never will be. He in time will return home, and forget you; and in the course of time you will be married, but not to Mr. Chick. Owing to the time and thought he devotes to you, he is not making the progress that he otherwise would; and you are hurting yourself, and would grieve your parents if they knew you were thus interested. Now, Mary, go to your mother, and make her your confidant. or stop just where you are. I take this unexpected way of reaching you, through the eyes of your uncle, for your good. I am Emeline Clap."

When I read this letter to my niece, who had written it without knowing what she had written, she listened to it somewhat dazed at the unexpected revelations of the contents, they being the secrets of her own heart, unknown to others. It seems the matter was a pleasant flirtation,—a sweet secret between two hearts, for the time being beating as one, and no eye watching them. There was an eye it seems, but it was invisible. It was not God's, but it saw in the night as well as in the day. It was the eye of a supervising or guardian spirit.

It was evident from the circumstances that she, though its amanuensis, was so interested in the manner of its production that she was wholly ignorant of what she had written, or the message would not have found a passage through from the land of light and beauty to the eyes of this shadowy writer.

I did not realize myself that the message, so definitely stated, was founded on fact. Noticing the young lady's embarrassment, I said: "Is there anything to this, Mary? Is there a Mr. Chick?" "Yes," said she, "he is a fine young man, I think everything of him." "Well," said I, "who is he?" She said: "He is a sophomore." It is hardly necessary to write on this point further; it tells its own story. I will add here that my niece lived in Providence, and in the neighborhood of Brown University.

I had never heard of Mr. Chick; the message to me was a revelation. I was as certain as day that Mary was not the author of the communication. What can it be then in the nature of things but what it purports to be? Emeline Clap,— whose body had been dead and buried a score or two of years, but whose spirit was alive and moving among the dear ones of earth, an interested observer, stepping into the current affairs of life and setting right, so to speak, a misplaced switch that possibly might have led to disaster. This interposition was effectual, the source of it more potent, perhaps, in working the cure than any earthly advice would have been.

I would like to understand this matter as anyone else would. I know where it is from as certain as I know where sunlight is from; but the why? Why this manifest interposition in this instance and not in the thousand other cases of as much and perhaps of more moment, that seem to have no supervising, viewless aunts? In this case was it accidental, the "Gates Ajar" of both worlds coincidently? It is of no use to speculate. There is the fact as it is and the circumstances, and seems to me it is clearly an intelligent spirit interposition. This, with more or less definiteness, seems to warrant me in feeling, as I have before said, that this "radiant maiden" who appeared to my sister at her earthly life's exit is the "white lady" of our house. May her shadow never be less, even if mine is; and now as a finish and a finis to this sketch, I will add the following anonymous lines, after thus proving them, I think, to be literally true: —

> "The living are the only dead;
> The dead live never more to die;
> And often when we think them fled,
> They never were so nigh."

XVI.

IDENTIFICATION OF SPIRITS.

The Sage of Galveston returns according to promise.

The positive identification of a spirit is one of the things seldom accomplished even by those who think they are getting tests. One of the prominent conversions to modern Spiritualism was made through, perhaps, an innocent deception on the part of a spirit, if deception, in any sense, can be innocent.

The fact was this: the spirit of a brother, who lived and died in Europe, manifested through a medium to his sister, who was visiting this country, giving his name and some family circumstances wholly unknown to anyone here,— not even known that she had a brother. It was an agreeable surprise, and was the means of making a Spiritualist of her, and a very prominent one. Later in her experience she learned directly that the spirit of her brother had never communicated, and that the spirit controlling the medium had read her mind, and fed her with what would be very naturally considered tests. They were tests of spirits, but not tests of identification. Good was done by even this deception. A valuable convert was made to the cause, and she is now one of the conspicuous speakers on its platform. I merely mention this to show how difficult it is to get unmistakable identifications, not to justify or qualify any deceptions, no matter the motive. I have had a few, as the reader of these "Shadows" will have seen, but not many that are unquestionable. I do not think identification of spirits the important thing in modern Spiritualism. It is very easy to get positive manifestations of spirits, and the fact that any spirit of a departed human being can come, good or bad, settles the fact, law, or principle; and if one spirit survives the death of his body, the law holds good for all.

I think it better that identifications should be difficult and seldom, otherwise we would depend too much upon the departed for aid and counsel, which would certainly retard human progress. I think no one who is zealously and honestly seeking for truth in this direction but will find now and then an identification of a spirit, but not often enough to make him perfectly happy, but often enough for his human good. That identifications are possible is an unmistakable fact. I think I will not enlarge upon the subject further in this chapter, the *rationale* of the matter not now being my principal object; but, with what I have said, I will relate a remarkable case of identification, where my friend, the "Sage of Galveston," as I used to familiarly call him, returned to me, according to promise, unmistakably.

I wrote an account of it, and printed it at the

time. The statement seems to express all the points
very clearly, so I will now print that instead of
rewriting it, and, perhaps, condensing it. It was
written as a fugitive article, and not with as much
literary care as I would have done if intended for
book-form, but I trust any superfluous rhetoric will
not be a blemish. It was necessary to be very particular and minute on the points in order to have the
whole matter understood. I consider the circumstance a very important one, and worthy of careful
perusal. The article referred to is as follows : —

> "Now came still evening on, and twilight gray
> Had in her sober livery all things clad."

Such was the fact to the world and to me on the
closing in of a pleasantly and busily occupied Sunday
in May (this was in the year 1881). I had laid
down my pen, and folded my notes and papers, and,
seeing a copy of "Paradise Lost" handy on the
table. I laid the book on them to keep them intact
during my absence, which was to attend a circle.
The book in question may have invited the draft of
the above quotation to begin with, or the man behind
the book; it is difficult to tell the exact factors of
inspiration, and I do not know, in this connection, as
it is of any consequence.

After a pleasant and somewhat thoughtful walk of
about half an hour, in which I took no note of time,
not even of its loss, I found myself at the medium's
door. This was Miss Shelhamer's home-circle evening, not for visitors, except on invitation, and I was

one of the privileged. It proved, indeed, a privilege, and enables me to corroborate the return of a friend whose name heads this article, and to say, also, it is one of the most perfect identifications of an individual spirit I ever had or ever heard of; and the circumstances in connection forbid any such explanation as mind-reading, or unconscious cerebration, as is often suggested, at least by those who strain at a gnat, in the spiritual manifestations, and swallow camels in other matters. Such perfect tests of identification as the one of which I am speaking are very rare, comparatively, among experiences, not as tests of spirits, but tests or proofs of identification, and, therefore, it is worthy of elaborate record; and that is my apology for the space I occupy.

I do not know as it is wise or sensible to begin as I have in this somewhat poetical manner; but it expresses the state of my feelings, and, may be, an impression; I do not say it is, but it reminds me of "Junius." Speaking of the eagle, he says: " The feather that adorns the royal bird sustains his flight; strip him of his plumage, and you pin him to the earth." I trust, then, the "plumage" of this article, if there should be any, will be forgiven. How much my occupation during the day had to do with the sentimentality of the hour, or how much it had to do with the fact that made this occasion a privilege, I will not undertake to say. I think we sometimes accidentally make conditions that are not always at our command on call; that is my apology now for being so minute.

The day had been wholly spent in my study,—my books, papers, pigeon-hole contents, and correspondence around me, and, to some extent, in me; it had been a sort of "washing-day" in my literary life. Our thoughts, you know, have queer ways of reaching us; autographic suggestions not only carry memories with them, but they carry presences also. How much, then, of my day's thoughtful occupation had to do with the connection made with my Texan friend I do not know; perhaps my condition was not in any sense a factor; but I feel impressed to begin in this way, and even to call to my aid, in the way, perhaps, of superfluous "plumage," the sweet, orphic lines of Emerson, in suggestion of connections that exist, that are not always *prima facie*, where the poet says:—

> "And on his mind at dawn of day
> Soft shadows of the evening lay;
> For the prevision is allied
> Unto the thing so signified.
> Or say, the foresight that awaits
> Is the same genius that creates."

Before giving the circumstances in connection with the communication that has inspired this article, I will first briefly speak of the man and his association with me, and our correspondential intimacy.

J. S. Thrasher, whose initials were autographically and typographically and indelibly during my life impressed on my mind as *I.* S. Thrasher, was a rare man, and, I think, had a toning influence on my style of expression. The initials of which I have spoken are an important item in this statement, and I shall refer to them again when I reach the proper place. I always called Mr. Thrasher, in my correspondence, the "Sage of Galveston," beginning my letters: "My Dear Sage," and, in return, I suppose, he always began his letters to me: "My Dear Philosopher." I became very much attached to him, and the attachment was mutual.

It began in this way: Something I had written had attracted his attention, and he wrote to me inquiringly, and the reply opened a correspondence which has not ended, it now seems, with his life in the form. I have a box — it is now before me — of about a cubic foot in dimensions, full of his letters to me. There are more bright thoughts, wise words, good advice, and common sense in them than can be found in any package of letters that I know of with an equal number of words. Our pen-acquaintance began in 1874. My attachment to him was not because he appreciated my articles, for he was much more of a critic than a patron. I used to think oftener of what he would say, when I was writing an article, than what the reading public would say; there was where he toned me up, and I have no doubt he is now saying: "Condense, John, condense," and I am going to after this; but, for reasons already stated, I want the privilege of superfluity now, for I feel that I am writing on an important matter.

The "Sage of Galveston," as I still like to call him, was a man of wide experience, and had led an active life, commercial, political, and literary. Some

twenty odd years ago he was on the editorial staff of
the *New York Herald*, occupying the position several
years. He was born in New England, but left it
when a young man. He lived at the South the latter
part of his life, beginning his residence there before
the late war; and when he came across my pathway,
as I have said, some six or seven years ago, he was
and had been long a resident of Galveston. He
was then a Spiritualist, had lost by death his wife
and children, so his home, in the ordinary sense, was
desolate. His aged mother lived with him, and she
seemed to be the only connecting link with this life.
He was singularly modest and retiring for so full a
man, and was very happy in his belief in Spiritualism. He had very thoroughly investigated it, and,
being satisfied, he stayed satisfied, living the life that
Spiritualism teaches, at least teaches theoretically.
I trust that some day, as our truth gets incorporated
into humanity more generally, there will be more
Thrashers living practical lives than now, so that it
will be less of a theory and more of a life.

The "Sage" had great practical common sense in
Spiritualism, as in everything else. He seemed to
know where he was going, when this life closed in,
more intelligently than most men that I have met,
and he has gone there; and now tells me, as his
"message" will show, that "he is quite comfortable." How natural was that easy way of saying it;
so like him, as the general tenor of that box of letters
will show. He put himself in the shape to take life
easy. Having made up his mind, in his lonely

domestic state, that commerce and enterprise would allure him no more, or disturb his mind, he invested his available means in an annuity that supported him generously, so that he could live to his liking, and have something for charity, and be hospitable, as many travelling Spiritualists can testify.

He often sent for mediums to visit him; they became residents at his house for longer or shorter periods, and great was the comfort he took in the manifestations at his own home and elsewhere. Even the account of them gladdened my heart. His experiences and wise conclusions have helped the stability of my own sensuous experiences. I do not mean that I needed his evidences to indorse mine, but it is so pleasant to find bright, scholarly, cultured minds in accord with one's own. He lived with the spirits; he seemed to fully realize that he had invisible company. As I have said, commerce and business, which once allured him, had no attractions for him, and, when he died, the competency he had died with him. I do not know as that was a wise investment, but I think it was wise for him. At any rate, when he died he was not weighted with the ballast of wealth that anchors so many spirits to earth after their bodies are dead and buried. It was, of course, a misfortune to have been left alone, death taking his family, but he felt always near them, and on many important occasions they were vividly manifest.

He visited the East once a year during the last three years of his life, and we were much together during these three visits. When last here, in the summer of 1879, he spent a few months in the western part of the State for his health, which was poor. He was then alone in the world, his aged mother having a few months before passed on, near fourscore-and-ten, and he seemed ready to go himself, and felt, and so did I, that he was near the end of the road; and when I bade him good-bye in the fall of that year, as he left for the South, he said, as he had said many times before, "*Au revoir*," meaning that he would manifest at the earliest opportunity, and report how he found things. He has now done so, at least in a measure, and to me, who have his letters, that tally with the tenor of his message, the report is ample and satisfactory, and I am glad he has been, and is to be, near me; I knew it before he said so. I am glad he proposes to communicate again, and perhaps continue, and thus, though the "river" divides us, we are not divided.

In getting the "true inwardness" of this identification the reader must permit me to refer again to his initials. He signed his name on his two or three hundred letters as I. S. Thrasher. Capital I's and J's in writing are often written alike, but in addressing his letters to me the J in John was a J, and came below the line, while the I or J in his signature did not, but was written exactly as he wrote the personal pronoun I, and I always superscribed my letters to him I. S. Thrasher. After a pen-acquaintance of about a year, I noticed his name printed in a list of small contributions in a newspaper, "I. S. Thrasher, Galveston, $3.00," and I became as perfectly satisfied

that his initial letter was an I as I am that mine is a
J. There was no occasion for settling the point, for
in all our correspondence he spoke of me as the Philosopher, and I addressed him as the Sage: "My
Dear Philosopher;" "My Dear Sage." The discovery that the initial letter was a J, as this article
is headed, is due to the fact that the spirit knew his
own name better than I did.

I have written a pretty long introduction or episode,
after leaving the reader at the door of Miss Shelhamer's house on that Sunday evening in May; but the
many words since written will enable me to be both
brief and intelligent in finishing up the corroboration.
I do not propose to present a record of that circle,
only that which bears on this subject. In the course
of the evening I had had an interesting and characteristic letter from the spirit of Ralph Huntington;
the control had also said that my daughter Hattie
and sister Adeline, my brother, father and father-in-
law were present; therefore, I had six friends among
the invisibles. The control afterwards said, addressing me: "There is a spirit who comes to you and
wants to be recognized; he died a good way off and
many months ago." I said: "Who is he? what is his
name?" "I will see if I can get it," said the control;
and after some hesitation said something that sounded
like Frasher, and John or James; but as I knew no
James, and no Frasher, I said: "Cannot some of my
spirit friends tell me his name?"

The spirit said he had tried hard to manifest, and
had promised me that he would, and the control said

he seemed disappointed and persevering. I said: "Tell the spirit to come to the *Banner* circle, and try to manifest there"; and the control said he would if he could. A little while after this, "Lotela" controlled the medium. She is an Indian spirit of a lively turn of mind, and she said: "Wetherbee chief, that spirit that knows you is here still, and wants to be recognized." I said I wanted the recognition as much as he did, and I was sorry I was so stupid. She then said: "I see four large letters right over him and you—S-A-G E." "Oh," said I, "the 'Sage of Galveston,' my friend Thrasher. He died some months ago, and promised to manifest to me when he went over, if he could."

The spirit was delighted to be thus recognized, and I still more so,—for it was so impossible for our acquaintance to have been known by the medium, and the cognomen of "Sage" was wholly correspondential and private. This was an extremely interesting affair to me; but the climax was the message that came from him shortly after at the *Banner* circle.

I went to the circle. I do not go often; have not the time; was detained down town one afternoon to meet a friend late, and so went to the circle to pass the time, and the message published in the last *Banner of Light* was given. Very few people—not more than one or two—in this city knew Mr. Thrasher, or of our close correspondential relations, and I do not believe a living soul in the world knows that he was in the habit of addressing me as "My Dear Philosopher," and that makes it a test. He refers to me, as will be seen by his message, as his friend and philosopher, and I can show over two hundred letters from him, beginning "My Dear Philosopher," or referring to me as his philosopher and friend, which is a feature in that message. The general contents, also, are such as to be unmistakably his to anyone who knew the tenor of our intercourse. Above and beyond this internal evidence is what I shall hereafter say of his message which frees the communication from any suspicion of mind-reading on the part of the spirit that would have made him, possibly, an *alias*.

Oh, how my heart died within me when he closed the message thus: "You may say it is from J. S. Thrasher, of Galveston, Texas, to his philosopher friend, John Wetherbee, of Boston." The J broke my heart. Everything else was perfect. I don't know what I would have given to have had that spoken an I, in giving his name, instead of a J. I felt and knew it came from my Galveston friend, but why spirits so often get twisted on some trifle that the man himself never would mistake if he were in the form, but a spirit often does, is one of the unaccountables.

There was no mistaking the message and the circumstances as being from my friend, the "Sage," but the J coming, intead of an I, led me into a careful investigation, and I spent three evenings carefully reading his letters, and, to my great joy, I found two of them out of the lot signed with a J. That settled all the other I's to be J's, and in one letter, where he was quoting something of mine, and putting his own version also, he put at the end of mine as author, J. W., and at the end of his, J. S. T. Before I had discovered the fact. I wrote South to a friend for information, and have received a reply that his initial letter was J, as his friend writes me in reply to mine, that his name was John S. Thrasher. So it seems the spirit was right, and I was wrong. If, on the evening that I spent at Miss Shelhamer's circle, I had known this — that his initial letter was a J — I would probably have made my connection with him more readily; and when the spirit was saying John and James, and approximating to a Thrasher by saying Frasher, I would not have had to wait for the "Sage" suggestion before I recognized him; but in the end it was all for the best.

I may not have succeeded in making this as clear as I could wish, as there is so much esoteric in its nature not convertible into exoteric without an unwarranted elaboration, but to me it covers the whole ground, and I must ask the reader to take the unspoken and unspeakable minutiæ on my say-so, and believe my *ipse dixit* when I say it is conclusive.

XVII.

Prime factors. — Philosophical musings on human happiness.

Modern Spiritualism, teaching as it does great duration to human existence, even conscious personality in perpetuity, it should teach us also how to insure the best conditions for such an existance, having an eye to happiness. As "one man's meat" — so the proverb says — "is another man's poison," so, in a sense, one man's happiness may be another man's misery. So I do not propose to write an essay on happiness, or on the conditions to insure it; but, being in a musing frame of mind, I will jot down a few thoughts that the subject seems to suggest.

I have had my happy hours and my sad hours. I suppose most everyone can say the same, but that need not hinder my saying it. Considering that my health through life has been remarkably good, I ought to score it on the side of happiness as a whole, and so I do. Human happiness, it seems to me, is mainly a constitutional quality. "Men," says Emerson, "are what their mothers made them;" that is, when a man is born the gate of gifts is closed. Pine may harden with care, or outward application, but it never can become oak, nor the latter, by any process, become pine. There is the same inherent differences in human nature. We can grow advantageously or disadvantageously by conditions, more or less at our command, but pine is always pine, and oak oak.

I know of a family of four children; they are adults or dead now; but, with my ideas, they are living, two in the form, and two as spirits; but I will use all four as an illustration, as I know them well, and they seem to fit my case. The oldest was born of a happy mother, whose years of grief had not arrived, and he manifested cheerfulness all his days, even under adverse circumstances. Misfortune came upon this family, and the second child, gestating under home sadness, was sad and pensive all her life; very fascinating, but soberly beautiful even in her adolescent years, she was not a diffuser of joy or sunshine, but was the product of her mother's condition.

The sun came out of the cloud again in that family, and the home was radient with light and joy, and the third child, born in that sunshine, was sparkling and bright, a joy in the house all her days, shedding happiness wherever she went. Then came trouble and misfortune to that family, and a broken household, and the fourth baby was a child of grief all his days. There were rises and falls in their several thermometers of happiness, but the tenor of their lives show correctly their ante-natal conditions. They all lived until at least the high noon of adult life, and two of them, as we have said, are still in the form, as elderly people. This episode will explain, without a long dissertation, what I mean when I say human happiness is more of a constitutional than an acquired quality.

With the foregoing remarks as an introduction, I will go on and say it takes a combination of qualities to make happiness, — we might say qualities innumerable. They can, however, be reduced to a few. We will call them "prime factors." People are very differently constituted; one often wanting what another possesses; but, we think, no one would make an entire change with another, our personality has such a perpetual interest in our being. We will let the poet express our thought instead of doing it ourselves, by quoting from Pope : —

> " Whate'er the passion, knowledge, fame, or pelf,
> No one will change his neighbor with himself.
> The learned is happy nature to explore;
> The fool is happy that he knows no more;
> The rich is happy in the plenty given;
> The poor contents him with the care of heaven."

This quotation is poetry, but I do not indorse it as even approximately true, but it is suggestive of truth.

While none are perfectly happy, and, of course, some are happier than others, we think it would be found, if there was any way of finding it out, that happiness is more equally divided than anything else in the distribution of gifts in human life; certainly more than in the great essentials, — such as

health, wealth, genius, or position. It will be a
rather arbitrary supposition; but suppose we fix the
number of "prime factors" of human happiness at
ten. This, however, is no more arbitrary than the
use of x for an unknown quantity, though I hardly
expect to find its value, like a sum in algebra, for
human nature is not a branch of mathematics as yet.

Though fixing the "prime factors" of human happiness at ten and definite, they necessarily blend,
run into each other, like the primary colors of a ray
of light. Disintegrated by the prism, these "prime
factors," just like colors, are often, and, necessarily,
complementary. The solar spectrum is a good analogous illustration of our point, human happiness
being the ray of white light. Apply the mental
prism to the ray of happiness, and the rainbow of life
stratifies into the supposed ten primaries, or "prime
factors;" or that is our scale or spectrum, for the
sake of lucidity, perhaps, as we have said, somewhat
arbitrary. We would designate them thus:—

1.	Goodness.	6.	Contentment.
2.	Health.	7.	Success.
3.	Hope.	8.	Popularity.
4.	Home.	9.	Social Position.
5.	Industry.	10.	Wealth.

Perhaps a little consecutive elaboration may be of
advantage here. What we mean by

Goodness, not religion, for a man may be religious
without being good; not virtue, but it includes that.
It means living for others as well as for one's self.

Many of the other factors of happiness are born of this one.

Health.—Parent of virtue. Without it all the ten spokes of the wheel of happiness rattle in their revolution. While one man with many gifts is lower in the scale of happiness, and another, with the same or less, is higher, the fact is due often to one's health. A man can afford to be marked low on many of the factors of happiness if health can be marked high thereby.

Hope is one of the great essentials of happiness. Hope without success (material or otherwise) is better than success without hope,—just as a rich poor man is happier than a poor rich man. Cheerfulness is one of the children of hope. Too much hope leads often to disappointment; but there is the compensation; it saves a soul from despair, and hides a multitude of sorrows. A man had better lose everything than hope.

" *Home*, sweet home, there is no place like home ! " when goodness, cheerfulness, and harmony abound. Blessed are they who have it. Money, popularity, or position is no substitute for it.

Industry.—Occupation, something to do, a disinclination to be idle. If success in the pursuits of life leads to rest or idleness, better remain poor and industrious, or die. Most men require the stimulus of active business or trade to keep them employed. With success they would be without occupation; an afternoon of rest is a life of unhappiness. It is better to be on a tread-mill than to rust.

Contentment is better than wealth. It is a constitutional rather than an acquired quality. To be satisfied is great gain. Happy are they who can look out of humble homes and cheap joys on palaces and equipage, and heave no sighs.

Success. — This word has no necessary relation to money or trade in this connection. A man may be a success without being a millionaire. Henry D. Thoreau was a success, though he died poor; so was Publicola; but Crœsus was not, nor many modern ones that could be named, though they had wealth. Who would not prefer to be Agassiz, without wealth, than Jim Fisk with?

Popularity. — Most people like to stand well with their fellows. Few are indifferent to approbation. One of the accented motives for gaining wealth is to impress others; to be in their eyes of some consequence. The popularity born of goodness and cheerfulness is more to be desired than that born of wealth. The former has a heavenly flavor, the latter an earthly one.

Social Position. — "A man's a man for a' that, and a' that." Worth makes the man, and not position. Still, hereditary competency, the refinements and comforts of genteel (not snobbish) life, are by no means small matters to be born into, or grow into. Patrician and plebeian have a recognized distinction: money will not buy the one, or the want of it impose the other.

Wealth is the grandest servant in life to a wise man. It is often a hard master, and keeps one

awake nights. The ninety out of the hundred have
to be happy without it; the ten who have it are not
always happy thereby. The problem is solved that
the most happiness, as far as this factor is concerned,
lies in the mean between poverty and wealth. Robert
Burns hints at the true idea when he says: —

> "Not for to hide it in a hedge,
>   Nor for a train attendant;
> But for the glorious privilege
>   Of being independent."

It is my opinion, as the truth of modern Spiritualism becomes incorporated in the mind of mankind,
in the same way as some of the other laws of nature
have,— not looking forward to a future life simply as
a matter of sentiment, but as a matter of fact, — it
will lead to a fairer distribution of what are called
the essentials in this life; mankind will tend to lay up
more enduring treasures than they do now,— those
that they can carry with them into the land of souls.
That certainly is the logic of the thought; the practical short-coming is the measure of a man's doubt
or belief.

XVIII.

ALLEN DOLE.

A reliable family tradition that amounts almost to a personal experience.

The following incident may be of interest enough to relate; at any rate it will not take long to do it. In my very early childhood there was an old relative of mine, whom I will call Allen Dole. I am not fully sure whether I remember him, or only think I do, having heard so much of him traditionally from the old members of our family. At any rate, he died when I was very young, and what I have to say of him would be traditional, whether I can recollect him, or whether the stories had been told so often that they had taken the form in me of experiences. It makes no difference, however, as what I am going to say is perfectly reliable, and told to me and spoken of before me, and continued to be spoken of by several of the old familiar faces of those days, even until I had almost reached manhood, so I relate it with all the confidence I would if it were my own experience, or if I had been one of those old folks myself.

As I have already written this circumstance out,

and printed it in an article on "Dormitory Thoughts" as one of the illustrations of the subject, I will copy it as therein written, instead of recomposing it.

The article referred to is as follows: —

"Who would have thought such darkness lay concealed
Within thy beams, O Sun! or who could find,
While fly, and leaf, and insect are revealed,
That to such countless orbs thou mad'st us blind!
Why do we then shun death with anxious strife?
If Light could thus deceive, wherefore not Life?"

Coleridge thought these lines the best in the English language. They may be; that is a matter of taste; but the thought conveyed in them is certainly both hopeful and suggestive, and so is a good introduction to what I have to say in this dormitory effort.

I think it will not be a digression if I relate an incident that has always interested me, and is not irrational by the view I take of sleep-life in these articles. A relative of mine, whom I will call Allen Dole, who died quite an old man when I was a youth, had, during his adult life, periodical spells of inebriation lasting a day or two, then followed months of creditable sobriety. Except for this one failing he was a very estimable man. When this irresistible thirst came on he had to have his spree, if it could be called one, for he knew when it was coming on, and deliberately prepared for it, passing the dark season quietly all by himself in his own room; hence his weakness was not generally known to the outside world.

On one occasion, coming among us after one of these retirements, he said he had had a very singular dream, which lasted a good while. "It was more than a dream," said he; "there was something unusually real about it." His brother knowing his habit, said: "Oh, you were only balmy, perhaps out of your head." Allen, finding a more hospitable disposition in the rest of us, related it, saying he felt then under its influence, as if he had just returned from a long journey. That was natural enough, we all thought, though we did not say so, but listened attentively to the narration of it, which was about as follows: —

"A person of angelic appearance came and awoke me and said; 'Allen, I want you to go with me.' I did not feel much surprised, and prepared to go as a matter of course. I was rather attracted to this visitant from the land of souls. I say this from what followed. I found myself moving along with this messenger,—without any mechanical effort I seemed to be gliding along, as it were, in his company. This movement seemed to excite in me no surprise nor expectation. I paid no attention to any surroundings; but as I call the vision now to my mind, I seemed to be in a misty or cloudy envelope, my companion, not my progress, being my attraction.

"After moving along in this way for some time, the misty surroundings having grown into a more beautiful light, my companion said to me: 'Here we are, Allen.' I don't know when our locomotion changed; but at this time we were walking quickly over the soft, velvet-like, grassy turf, and it seemed to be now the auroral splendor of a new and magnificent morning, and all the landscape was in harmony with it. It seemed to be the most beautiful place I was ever in, and, while feasting my eyes on the natural attractions of the locality, I found I was in the midst of a large gathering of very happy people. It seemed to be a festival. I felt and breathed pleasure in the happy atmosphere that environed me. I felt at home, —that is, I did not feel like a stranger, nor did these happy people seem to consider me one, or as a new comer. The situation, as I now think of it, seems strange to me, but it did not then.

"One thing was very singular, but even that excited no surprise; the faces of all these people were the faces of the departed, the vanished lights of human life, the still living forms of the loved and lost. Some of them had died before I was born; but I knew who they were just as well as I did those who had been the remembered faces of by-gone days, and many of them were those whom I had followed to the grave; but they were all alive, as much so as I was then, myself. But what surprises me now is that, finding all these dead faces alive, it did not surprise me then. There was Lucinda (who had died about a year before), not the emaciated young woman that consumption had had so long in its grasp, but the picture of health and youthful activity. In the words of the poet : —

"It did not seem irrational, or queer,
    To thus confabulate in common speech
  With this old friend who had been dead a year,—
    Strange things these dreams, and sometimes wisdom teach."

"Not one of my living friends was there; not one of you" (addressing us). "If I had met any living faces there, I do not think they would have seemed strange to me any more than it did to be there myself; but if I had, and remembered the fact now, as I do the vision, or dreamy experience, I should consider it ominous, or prophetic of dissolution. I would feel now that that person was soon to be called home."

This is enough to relate of Allen's account. There were other details of no general interest, so I will only add that after Allen had been there what seemed quite a long time, his mother, who, with others, was very near him, said it was time to go; but Allen was reluctant; said he preferred to stay. She said: "No, you must go now; but in fifteen years you will come again, and then stay all the time, like the rest of us." I will add that Allen died in about fifteen years. It was always said by aunt Fales, whose memory was good on superstitious matters, that he died exactly fifteen years from the date of that vision. If that was the case, or even if only an approximation, there was prevision, as well as method, in the circumstances of that somewhat singular dream, which, as Allen said, was something more than a dream.

I do not know as this traditional family incident has any general bearing on the subject of this book of "Shadows," unless to make it more in keeping with its title; yet a matter — whether dream or vision — occurring near a century ago, and fifty years almost before the advent of modern Spiritualism, and giving a picture of the future life so different from the

notion prevalent at that time, and so in keeping with
the teachings of modern Spiritualism, that it at least
is a pointer, even if the prophetical part of it may
have been a little strained.

The circumstance so believed in by the old
people of our house, who have long since passed
beyond the vale, made quite an impression upon me,
as one of the facts in my early life. I think, also,
modern Spiritualism has somehow tended to keep the
old familiar faces of by-gone days in more close
remembrance than if I had believed that dead people
were dead when they had "shuffled off the mortal
coil." With some such ideas as I am expressing
now, I put the foregoing incident into simple verse
a long time ago, which I will add for the sake of
making this chapter of a respectable length, although
it is a repetition of what has been already told in the
foregoing account : —

Here in this churchyard's melancholy shade
   Sepulchral stones stand thickly planted round;
My wandering footsteps hitherward have strayed
   To read the names of tenants under ground.

The dove there perched on yonder slab oblique,
   Swerved from its line by many a frosty year,
Seems sensing sentiment it fain would speak,
   And accents well the thought to wanderers here.

On that same slab was chiseled "Allen Dole;"
   The year he died, his death also, and age :
The grass was pulled aside to read the whole,
   But nothing found of his illumined page.

That was not written on this old grave-stone,
   Where crawling ivy covers it from sight,

But told in solemn words to me alone
   How Allen saw the world of spirits bright.

Now day is closing for the coming night,
   And memories sad, like phantoms, come and go;
The dove has flown; the fire-flies show their light,
   With thoughts of people whom we used to know.

With evening, shadows come of actions done
   In hours when sunlight leaves no passing trace;
But retrospection calls back one by one,
   And gives in sober thought to each its place.

In dim forgetfulness, how apt to hide
   The selfishness that marks most all our acts!
But in this evening hour their shadows glide
   Unbidden to the mind,—the naked facts.

But Allen flanked this thoughtful evening school:
   A glass of rum in him made evening day;
So all the morning hours he'd play the fool,
   Driving reflection's warning voice away.

But Allen's cares increased as time unrolled:
   His early life grew indistinct with years,
And manhood's record blurred as he grew old,—
   He found the world at last a vale of tears.

Then hearken well! The hour will come to all,
   When time, so fleeting, whispers "sands are low!"
Few may forecast, and anxious wait the call,
   As Allen did, who, smiling, said " I go."

But Allen grieved not as he neared fourscore,
   Though friends were few, and end of days so near;
For he had been upon that other shore,
   And talked with angels in their happy sphere.

Once Allen saw his body sound asleep!
   Perhaps 't was rum that dualized his sight?
He saw the angels who their vigils keep
   While others led him to that world of light.

O beauteous sky and rainbowed atmosphere!
   The grass was soft and frescoed bright with flowers;
The air so balmy,— music soft and clear
   Mingled with all.   Oh, happy, joyful hours!

He saw that face who watched his infant years,
   And other loved ones, buried long ago;
Brightly transfigured everyone appears;
   Frail Susan, also, whom he used to know.

They moved a slide, and let him have one sight
   Of that dread place called "spirit-quarantine,"
Where sinners stay whole ages, dark as night,
   To expurgate the beast from man divine.

They told him then that he must homeward go;
   But Allen felt inclined to linger there:
To save the quarantine, they let him know,
   'T were better to deodorize elsewhere.

They said to Allen, who was fifty-five,
   That fifteen years would fill his earthly score;
His seventieth year would find him just alive,
   The hungry graveyard knocking at his door.

Why should this man be blest with such a sight
   While saints go mourning all their days of earth?
We cannot judge.   God doeth all things right;
   Perhaps old Allen's thirst was heritage from birth.

Then draw the veil, should profanation seek
   To read the list of Allen's reckless days;
But let his later living record speak
   How spirit-quarantine reformed his ways.

Now thoughtfully our footfalls homeward bound,
   And homeward, also, to eternal light;
While here night's mantle overshades the ground,—
   We wait expectant for a world that's bright.

XIX.

INDIAN–SPIRIT INFLUENCES.

*What the subject suggests, and a supplement of poetry.
—Astronomical.*

One of the noticeable features in the phenomena of modern Spiritualism is the prominence it gives to the departed Indian race. There is hardly a medium in this whole Endoric class that is not more or less guided by, controlled by. or indebted to the departed Oseolas, Black Hawks, Red Jackets, Violets, or Blueflowers of that singular aboriginal people that once covered, in their wild and natural way, this North American Continent. I have sometimes thought, as this spiritual movement, in its modern aspect, is of American genesis, that one of the prime factors, perhaps the accented one that has made this modern connection with mortals in the form, was the influence and power of the Indian element in its departed, invisible, but still living form.

I am aware that history indicates that, if these phenomena be the influence of the spirits of departed human beings, though called modern, they are quite an ancient affair; but, in its uninterpreted state, was kept in the domain of either superstition or revelation, but only in this age has it been recognized as intelligent sensuous phenomena.

I am inclined to think, as I have said, that we are very much indebted to the Indian element in the spirit world for the light that was intelligently revealed to us in 1848. Perhaps owing to the natural way they lived when in the form, it gave them a strength or power that a more artificial life would not, so that even in spirit life one can say that "it is an ill wind that blows no one any good," and thus we are the gainers.

If the conditions had been right, and man had been hospitable to its advent, the witchcraft of two or three centuries ago, abounding so much in Europe and in this country, might have staid and been modern Spiritualism long ago, instead of waiting for our day. But the reception of it was such that the influences paused, and the light (or darkness, if you choose to call it so) was withdrawn. I am no particular lover of the Indian in the form, or in the raw material, so to speak, but I am ashamed of my race for treating it as it has, and I find a growing admiration for that fast-departing race, especially in its spiritual life, for the loving and forgiving disposition it has manifested in its invisible dealings with us.

I am not attempting any elaboration of this Indian feature of our *ism*, but am only too glad to recognize its importance in this matter in general, and their individual importance as guides, body-guards, or controls of the mediums that figure so largely in this modern movement.

I was once asked by a well-known medium — a doctress — to write her a poem for her to read at her anniversary, soon to take place. She said Saucy Jack, one of her controls, wanted me to. I make no pretensions in the poetical direction, but wishing to do both her and the invisible Indian a favor, I said I would try to do so. "Oh, you will do it," says she; "Saucy Jack says so." I soon after tried to write something, and succeeded in slowly working out some fifty lines. It was rather hard work, but I thought it would answer.

I met the lady accidentally a few days after, and asked her when she wanted the poetry, and to let me know in season, so that I could find time to write it, and have it ready for her. She spoke right up, and said: "Chief, what do you say that for, when you have already written it, and you have got it now in your pocket?" Well, such was the fact; it was, certainly, a pretty good guess. I think myself, the fact of her saying that the Indian control said I would write it, had some effect in stimulating me, as I always want the influences to be right when possible. I called it

THE INDIAN PEACE-WHOOP.

Wand'ring in dreams, in mazy rev'rie lost,
A feeling strange came o'er me. Tempest tossed,
Then calm, and then — a light upon me broke.
I heard a voice! And thus the spirit spoke:
"Knowledge is power!" we hear the white man say;
And, lo! he proves it. We the tribute pay

Of home, of life, of race. Slowly we yield,
And leave the white man master of the field.
No more the wigwam, squaw, or brave is seen,
Though streams still run, and hills and vales are green.
O'er this broad land the white race rules supreme;
It is his hour. But Red Man is our theme.
Has pale chief all the knowledge, all the power?
All nature's secrets, animal and flower?
We are big med'ciue braves; we have our sense,
And still are with you, although driven hence.
Our hunting-ground, invisible to you, is near;
Some hear our whispers, indistinct, or clear.
Having the power, through simple modes of life,
We reach you, white man, forgiving ancient strife;
Would do you good, would cure the aches and pain
That flesh is heir to,—thus good health obtain.
The red man in the form, with instinct blind,
Oft sensed a truth that culture failed to find.
As close to earth the Indian puts his ear
To sense the footfalls too far off to hear,
Or tread of game, or find perhaps the trail,
Gaining knowledge where higher outlooks fail,
Deep lessons inexpressible in speech,
And thus a royal road to knowledge reach.
"Knowledge is power," in whispers soft and low
Say we, and prove it, as our records show.
We reached humanity in your grandsire's day,
Aided by spirits bright; they showed the way;
We had the strength. Then mortals were possessed,
As witches burned, and other ways distressed.
Liking our sensitives, we soon retired,
And waited till our service was desired.
Thus came a solstice to this "Dawning Light."
Again we come, conditions being right,
To manifest to you this glorious truth:
That death is life, and age immortal youth.
We, red-skinned souls, to nature fondly drawn,
Are doing work as spirits of the morn;
And mediums all are strengthened by our aid,

And better manifestations now are made.
Blest be the form, when aided by our race,
That made it possible in this age to trace
Intelligent connection in spirit life
With lover, brother, sister, friend, or wife,
Whom you thought dead, and thus have found
That no man ever moldered under ground.
Then o'er the wide earth let the "Peace-Whoop" sound,
The spirits have triumphed! the lost are found!

Feeling as I do, and have said, that the Indian element is an important factor in the Genesis as well as the Exodus or going forth of modern Spiritualism, the fact has associated them in my mind with the advent of what has been poetically and appropriately called the "Dawning Light." As the anniversaries of this event come round every thirty-first day of March, the Indian seems to be a figure in the picture, though not always brought into the foreground. I have therefore thought it might not be out of good taste, while running thus a little into poetry, to add one at the close of this Indian chapter that was written for one of these anniversaries. I will print it as I find it in the report of the proceedings of March 31, 1882, as follows: —

The chairman then introduced to the people, John Wetherbee, of Boston, who spoke as follows: —

FRIENDS,—Expecting to be asked to say a few words on this occasion, I have come prepared with a short poem. I am no improviser, and I am no poet; but I thought I would follow my impression, and take the consequences.

I have put together a few fragmentary thoughts

suggested by the "Dawning Light" of 1848. I might call them "Night Thoughts," for their genesis was in the night. "Star Thoughts," perhaps, would be better, for when one thinks of the auroral hour of our Light, his thoughts are apt to have a heavenly or celestial twist in them, and we wander among the constellations,—at least I do. This is my preface, as well as my apology for what follows: —

> The "Dawning Light" of eighteen forty-eight
> The saints of earth have met to celebrate;
> Or some of them to thus commemorate
> This great prevision of our future state,—
> That man was not beneath the sod to wait,
> In a dead or decomposèd state,
> But pass at once through the celestial gate,
> Into the "Beyond," or "Evergreen Shore,"
> The "Sweet By-and-Bye," to die no more,
> Finding our departed friends awaiting,
> With outstretched arms, congratulating
> Us on our arrival from this world of sorrow
> Into the "Summer-Land" of death's tomorrow.
> This, then, was the telephonic story
> That made the "Dawning Light" a day of glory.
>
> Under the inspiration of this thought,
> So hopeful, and with such a future fraught,
> A feeling strange came o'er me, on my pen;
> My thoughts were more on angels than on men.
> Well, let it be so, 't is their sacred hour;
> They did the work, they had the mystic power.
> While being thus celestially inclined,
> My eyes were skyward turned, as well as mind;
> This globe of earth seemed like a palace-car;
> More than that,— I was riding on a star.
>
> > Is the earth a palace-car?
> > Are we riding on a star?

Ask the man on Venus bright:
Watchman, tell us of the night!
Who with wonder gazes high,
Sees our planet in his sky,
Bright as Venus at its best;
We shall need no other test;
We *are* riding fast and far,
We *are* trav'ling on a star.

Thou incandescent orb! Most glorious sun!
Holding this star, our world, fast in its course,
As one will sometimes swing with a string
A ball round and round, centripetally tied;
The tension, resisting gravitation,
Is the force centrifugal.   Thus balanced
Has this old star rolled on through space; no pause
Nor change since the stars sang their morning song.
Thus earth's relation to the god of day.
This line, holding the earth steady in place,
Though invisible, immaterial force,
Is firm and enduring, in length counting
Almost a hundred million miles, the sweep
Circumferential six hundred million.
Thy daily task, old star, then counts in miles
A million, yes, plus half a million more,
Before thy daily work is done; then day
By day the same to make the year complete;
And we are riding on this star sublime.

Thou bright, planetary neighbor! tethered
Like a dory to our ship,—silver-faced moon,—
Wert thou full six times further off than now,
Our star would span the distance in a day.
Where now beheld coquetting with the clouds,
In four short hours our speed would reach the spot.
Thirty miles an hour would steam-car travel
Continuously a year to do this four hours' work.
Thus hast thou sped, old earth, since time began.
Thy genesis with its misty morning

No man can date, but thy swift exodus
He can compute, and in more than fancy
Knows that he is traveling on a star.

  Is the earth a palace car?
  Are we riding on a star?
  Ask the man on Venus bright:
  Watchman, tell us of the night?
  Who with wonder gazes high,
  Sees *our* planet in *his* sky,
  Bright as Venus at its best;
  We shall need no other test;
  We *are* riding fast and far,
  We *are* traveling on a star.

This star, our earth, so quickly flying,
Carrying its more than billion passengers,
Or precious freight of human beings, jumps
Never its track. No misplaced switch ever
Leads our star parabolically astray,
Nor telescoped by swifter-speeding orbs,—
Never collision with inward-bound stars.
So steady and even has been the speed,
Though moving in its track two thousand miles
While quickest locomotive travels one,
That mankind at ease seems standing still,
Yet all the time is riding on a star.

Thus would we realize in solemn words
That we are moving with electric speed,
Yet slow compared with light, which moves
Ten thousand times as fast; and thought beats light,
And spirits travel on the wings of thought.
While our star, the earth, through space is moving
Thus its thousand miles and more a minute,
Other bodies are traveling also, each with
Its own right of way on their several tracks.
There are also wandering, harmless systems,
Streams of granulated, cosmic matter,
In revolutions sweeping round the sun.

At times old earth, the star on which we ride,
Goes through these cosmic systems with a rush.
The atmospheric clothing of our globe
Protects us, but the friction from its speed
Makes incandescent the granulations,
And they fall in harmless dust, and blazing
Meteors irradiate the midnight sky,
While we are riding on this star sublime.

An impression came to the star-eyed sage
As he reached this line on his written page,
Where many an hour he had wasted ink
To strike an idea that would make men think,
And during the time had traveled so far
Without being joggled, though riding a star,
That there might be zones in the realms of space
That vitalized thought in the human race,
The contact affecting humanity's dream
Something like sailing through the old Gulf Stream,
Where water is warm to one's physical sense;
But these zones warm soul with their influence.
Thus ages of light, or revivals of thought,
Have dawned on the world as history has taught;
For mankind's movements seem in waves to flow,
Some mountains high, and some are leveled low,
More like influence from an outside source,
That wakes stagnation into active force,
Perihelions, perhaps, in a spiritual sense,
Where influence divine is more intense.

Thus while riding on a star,
Traveling very fast and far,
Old earth entered somewhat so,
Four and thirty years ago,
The zone of the " Dawning Light,"
That made the conditions right,
And enabled angels bright
To make their presence felt;
Messages from raps were spelt,

Which, interpreted and read,
Broke the silence of the dead,
Thinned the curtain of our fate,
Forecasted our future state.
Man need not have traveled far
To have found the "gates ajar,"
For the spirit world was near,
Our departed still were here.
But the transit through this "zone"
Made the earth a telephone,—
Made sensitive the inward ear,
And silent voices vocal, clear;
Peopling the circumambient air
With living beauty everywhere.

Thus we celebrate the date,
March thirty-first, 'forty-eight,
As the genesis of our Thought,
That has golden luster brought
And marked the age with glory.
Is it out of place to say
(While moving through the Milky Way,
Or Galaxy of stellar light,
That spans so visibly at night
The great concave overhead)
Again the words already said,—
Is not earth a palace car?
See us riding on a star.
Ask the man on Venus bright:
Watchman, tell us of the night?
Who with wonder gazes high,
Sees our planet in *his* sky,
Sees it traveling fast and far,
While we are riding on the star.

XX.

A WAYSIDE SKETCH.

*An entertaining sketch that will fill up some deficiencies
in the course of these " Shadows."*

Sometimes I think the dear public of skeptical
people are often more deceived, their credulity taxed,
than are the body politic of spiritualistic believers.

The credulity is on the side of the opposition rather
than with us. I am sure I have been astute, eye-
opened, and expert in the investigation of this subject.
I have seen, of course, attempts to cheat by at least
supplementing their powers by more or less imposition; not always meaning to do anything very wrong,
but, perhaps, to give more for the fee received than
the spirits can do through them.

It has always been my wish, and so has it been the
wish of Spiritualists generally, that mediums would
have no manifestations rather than to have fictions,—
give it up as a failure, want of proper conditions, or
whatever the cause may be; but never to allow one's
mediumistic elasticity to stretch into anything of
their own doing; in the long run, people who do generally come to grief.

There are a great many people who are in the show department of this business, often having more or less mediumistic power, who find it more profitable to cater for the opposition rather than the spiritualistic public. It is a matter of dollars and cents with them. I could name a man who is a good medium for physical manifestations, but likes the popularity and the remuneration that he gets from the skeptical world better than poverty with truth. I have proved his mediumship when *incog.*, under crucial test conditions, and I have said to him, after making myself known : " Why do you go about exposing it, or mixing fiction extravagantly with fact, and call them spiritual manifestations?" He said in reply : " It is wholly a matter of dollars. If I should go into a village and do honest work as a spiritual medium, I could not get enough to pay my expenses ; but if I plan for the opposition, the religious class, the Christian Association, or the fashionable, to expose or bring discredit on it, I can get a full hall, and go away with money in my pocket."

I have been many times to see these paying exhibitions, and have seen many of the religious, literary, and official lights of the community sold, as the saying is, more than ever I saw a spiritual gathering sold, and I have been both amused and grieved to see a large audience of respectable and intelligent people humbugged into supposing they were witnessing the spiritual manifestations that have converted people to the cause. I have felt sorry, being a Spiritualist, to find that so many people were ready to think that that is the pabulum or sensuous phenomena that has attracted and retained me as one of the believers.

I was once traveling in the far, far West, and on the western slope of the Rocky mountains, and happened to be stopping in a mining town, where one of these shows of big spiritual advertisements had been going on; an interesting colloquy or circumstance occurred, which was quite amusing. I wrote an account of it over the signature of "Shadows," and that account I will add to what I have already said, as a finish to this chapter. If some part of it has been already recorded in this book, in the form now presented, it will hardly be a repetition. Pebbles, you know, become jewels by an appropriate setting; but the "repetition," or fact mentioned, is a jewel, setting or no setting; so, if it gets a new hearing, the reader will be all the better for it. The article is as follows : —

A traveler, very early in the morning, stopped at the tavern in Nevada City. He had come during the night in the branch railroad from Colfax, and registered his name. It was an hour or two before the guests were stirring. Those who looked at the register afterwards, as people are apt to, particularly in a suburban town, read the name of "Shadows," Colfax. As soon as breakfast was ready, this new comer, "Shadows," of Colfax, was more than ready, after an all-night ride, and immediately began sipping his hot coffee; and, before the guests had begun to gather much around the table, he had finished his meal, and was again comfortably sitting by the stove.

This stove was in the center of what might be called the office, as the bar was in the side room on the left, and the dining room was on the right, some conveniences in the rear, and this office seemed to be the general lounging room. This room was quite large. On one side was the clerk's counter and desk, and large piles of trunks on the other side; but they did not crowd it any. It was roomy, dirty, and comfortable. This stranger, seated by the stove, seemed to be in a brown study, taking no notice of anything or anybody. Not so the guests, as they came one after another out of the dining room, some to stop, others in passing gave a look at the stranger, and wondered who he was; the register gave his name. They who looked read "Shadows,"— the place where he hailed from, "Colfax"; but that was no definition.

Many, as usual on a cool morning, took seats around this stove. Of the eight or ten who occupied that position, some were young, some middle aged, some were old,—not very old nor very young. In a provincial place or mining town, as this was, a man of 60 looks easily 70, because the metropolitan style was lacking, and slouches more in order than stiff hats; and white shirts, though possibly in a majority, were not unanimous. It was a place where dress did not make the man, nor want of it the fellow. Old and young among the sitters looked more or less at the stranger, and all showed inquiring minds or faces, as if they wanted to ask him who he was, and what he was there for, and seemingly knowing no one. The stranger, however, gave no signs of explaining himself,— seemed perfectly at ease, and busy with his own thoughts.

Soon, however, the companions of the stove began to be sociable, still with an eye now and then on the stranger, to see, perhaps, if he thawed out any. They soon came to the conclusion that their talking or looking was quite indifferent to him. In the course of the general talk it seemed that some persons had created quite a sensation the Sunday evening before. filling the largest hall in the town to witness their wonderfully advertised spiritual manifestations. The parties were Eva Fay and a Mr. Bidden, I think. No Spiritualist who reads the newspapers would take any stock in them.

In listening to this general talk, and their several comments, *pro* and *con*, one could have got a tolerably fair account of what occurred at that entertainment, and, as it will be seen, this stranger did; but he gave no signs of interest; and whether he was listening or not, the strangers did not know. He certainly appeared to be deep in thought, living in a different world from them.

One of the younger members of the group, and one who talked more than his share, and might be described as a "bar-room boss," summed it all up by saying "it was a big humbug;" and I guess he was right, only he intended his "big humbug" to cover the whole subject from beginning to end, there and elsewhere. An old man (who used a crutch, having fallen from a rock), taking his pipe out of his mouth, said: "I do not think so; some of it may have been, but some of the things were really honestly done." "I do n't think Prof. Crosby took any stock in them, and he is a Spiritualist," said another. At the name of Crosby, the stranger looked at the party, but, in an instant, he was indifferent again. Some had noticed the look, and brought Prof. Crosby's name more to the front in this connection, but it had lost its charm, and the conversation subsided again into the subject of spiritual manifestations generally.

The young man, who we said seemed to sum it all up as a big humbug, said then, in a very positive way, that "Spirits have nothing to do with this folderol. All the things we read of as being done all over the country, and called spiritual manifestations, are all frauds." "Oh, that cannot be," said another. But the "boss," who seemed to know it all, and had seen it all — nothing more for him to learn — said: "I admit some of it to be true; but no spirits; it is electricity and mesmerism and mind-reading. All the rope-tying, rings put onto connected arms, slate-writing, tipping of tables, bell-ringing, are all deception, sleight-of-hand, or adroitness. Do you not see, said he, "how large their wrists are, and hands small?" This young man was very positive; spoke as if used to carrying his point in that crowd, as if those listeners were in the habit of being convinced by his saying so. All the argument need not be expressed in this wayside account. The reader will get about the situation from what has been related, this young "boss" of words being particularly happy in clinching his argument with electricity, mesmerism, and mind-reading.

The stranger turned his eye on this positive and fluent talker, and said in a bright, cheerful, but very deliberate manner: "My friend, will you define electricity? What is it?" The suddenness of the question embarrassed the young man a little, and he made, at first, no reply. All the listeners were as much interested in the stranger's breaking silence as in the question. The young speaker seemed to be aware that it was very easy to say it was electricity, but not so easy to tell what electricity was. The party all looked at the stranger, who, at last, had opened his mouth, and, after the pause mentioned, said to the young man: "You need not try to answer the question. The best that can be done by anyone is to say it is a mode of motion. Farraday once said, in reply to a question put to him: 'I suppose I know as much about electricity as anyone, and I am unable to say what it is, or define it.' If Farraday was dumb, it is no discredit to you to be dumb on the subject also. The spiritual manifestations may be electricity, as you say; but, to say so, is no explanation."

The young man, not wishing to lose any of his prestige in his own field, said to the stranger he had more in his mind mesmerism than electricity. The stranger at once said: "Well, my friend, what is mesmerism?" He replied: "The influence one mind has upon or over another, sometimes controlling it." "That is correct," said the stranger;" and added: "Is it the mind or the body that mesmerizes or controls the subject?" The young man said, rather hesitatingly: "The mind." "Of course," said the stranger, "for a body without a mind, or a corpse, would have no mesmeric power. I think," continued the stranger, "that Spiritualism is mesmerism." The young man began to feel as though he had an ally.

The stranger then said: "As the body cannot, of itself, mesmerize without a mind, is it not probable that mind can without a body?" "I never saw one, or ever heard of one," said the young man; and the sitters around the stove were interested and amused. "Well," said the stranger, "there are a great many things that exist that we cannot see, or intelligently perceive. We cannot see electricity or mesmerism. We know them only by their effects. We do not see minds or spirits; we know them by their effects. You have taken, my young friend, an electric shock, or seen one taken, and so you know electricity exists; some day, if you are lucky, you will have a spiritual shock; then you will have evidence of the other."

The young man said, in reply to the stranger: "A man may exist, after his death, with thinking powers, but I do not believe it. I am willing," said he, "to be convinced; I would like a spiritual shock here and now." "Well," said the stranger, "if I were a 'machine,' and conditions were right, I would give you one; but, as I am not, I will tell you of one I had myself. I have had a great many. This that I now refer to is so perfectly unmistakable that, if you

believe me, you will have to be convinced. I do not
expect, however, you will be convinced; the subject
is a matter of experience rather than of argument."
The stove-surroundings seemed desirous for an account of the stranger's first shock, so he gave it substantially as follows : —

"A niece of mine, a young lady of sixteen, said to
me during a visit at my house : 'Uncle, are you still
a Spiritualist?' I replied: Yes. She then related
something rather strange that had occurred in her
presence. I said: Molly, you must be a medium;
come and sit with me at this table. She did so, and
we tried for raps, or tips, but did not succeed. I
then put a pencil in her hand to hold, and, seeing a
motion, I put a sheet of paper under it, and her hand
made up and down motions, dotting the paper, but
no writing. The movement was strange to her, as it
was wholly involuntary. I then put the end of my
index-finger on the wrist of the hand that held the
pencil,— nothing more,— and her hand began to
write line after line, she saying: 'How queer, uncle;
I do n't do that; why, see, it goes of itself, and my
hand wont stop.' In this way she filled the page,
which I took, and she went right on writing the next
while I was reading the first, and it was the beginning of a wise, intelligent letter.

"While writing in this way, she was all the time
talking excitedly to me, often saying: 'Only see it,
uncle, and I am not doing it' (and the young man
smiled, as if he was thinking to himself: 'How she
was fooling the old man'). She ended the commu

nication by signing the name of an old aunt of mine who had died nearly fifty years ago, when my sister, the mother of this young lady, was a child, and this niece had never heard of such a person. So far, knowing that this young lady was honest, it was tolerable proof of the action of a spirit."

The young man said: "That is the way with all you folks. That would not suit me; that may have been all pretence. I do not say it was, Mr. Shadows, but it was possible; and, certainly, if there is any way of accounting for a thing naturally, no one will suggest the supernatural." "But, listen to me," said the stranger; "what do you think this letter was? It was from an invisible and watchful intelligence, who wrote in this way: 'You' (this young lady) 'are doing yourself and the young man an injury; the flirtation that you are now carrying on with that young college student, Mr. Chick, is highly improper, and will do an injury to both of you; it will amount to nothing. Both of you are too young, and you will both in time find your proper mates. Your mother would not like it, if she knew it; and now as I' (this invisible relative) 'am watching over you, I feel it my duty, as I love you, Molly, to have trifling ended. You must end it, or go to your mother and confide in her, who now knows nothing of it. I take this way of reaching you, and it shows you have friends watching you, whether you wake or whether you sleep.'"

The stranger said he told this from memory, and it was the substance of a long letter written auto-

matically, in the way described, by this young lady.
The nature of it is proof of its abnormal character.
I knew what she was writing before she did, otherwise she never would have allowed me to see it.
The young lady burst into tears from mortification
to see her inmost thoughts thus exposed. I said:
"Who is this Mr. Chick? Is there any such person? She said: 'He is a nice young man, who is in
college in our neighborhood, and I love him very
much.' Suffice it to say," said the stranger, "the
young lady learned a wise lesson that she has never
forgotten. There are eyes that see us and watch us,
and the knowledge of that fact, I may as well add,
is what the world needs more than it needs anything
else."

The young man had to own up that this was a remarkable case, as the stranger had stated it. "But I
have had," said he, "no such experience myself, and
I cannot believe it. I might have been saved from
much trouble if anybody's aunt had written a letter
to me. You are a stranger," said the young man;
"you tell a good story. I do n't want to doubt you,
sir, but it smells to me fishy. Perhaps I would think
otherwise if I knew you; but I would have to have
the experience myself. This may be a 'spiritual
shock' to you, but it has not shocked me a bit; and,
if I had been present, I feel pretty sure it would not
have struck me."

At this moment in walked Prof. Crosby from the
dining-room. The stranger's back was towards him.
He had heard a few of the last words of the confab,

and the stranger turning to see who had entered, the professor rushed towards him, saying : "Good God, John, where did you come from?" and he introduced the stranger to the persons around him as his friend "Shadows," of Boston.

It only remains for me to say that I wanted to surprise my friend, and, finding myself within a few hours' ride from him, thought I would make him a visit. I have no doubt, also, I instructed as well as entertained the members of the tavern office in that colloquy, and I think it was a fortunate circumstance that the "stranger" happened to be present. I think that Miss Fay is a medium, but I do not think her shows are any credit to Spiritualism. But the cause was not hurt any by the light that the "stranger," now known as "Shadows," cast upon the subject.

XXI.

MATTER AND SPIRIT.

Of intercourse with spirits. — Some conditions worth knowing. — Illustrations — Sealed letters.

It is the opinion of many able writers, including the late Robert Dale Owen (who had wide experience in dealing with the spirits, and did so very advantageously), that spirits do not see material objects, or hear material sounds, as we mortals do. From my own experiences, I agree with him and them that it requires material organs to see material objects and hear material or external sounds. In one sense, sounds may not be strictly material; for instance, the human voice, — that is, an external expression of the human spirit, but it is material in its manifestation from its impulse to its expression. It is air vibrations, and air is material. It requires the auricular organ to hear a sound; by and through that organ it reaches the sensorium, and becomes a matter of consciousness. So, also, it requires the optical organ to see a material object, and through it the object reaches the sensorium, and becomes a matter of consciousness or perception.

This seems very simple talk on very common, simple things. Optical and auricular organs are so common, born with us, and are in practical use from infancy to age with no effort on our part. The operation is so simple that, as a matter of course, the *modus operandi*, and the philosophy of the phenomena of perception is rarely thought of. Yet, simple and common as it is, no one, no matter the extent of his knowledge, however much of a scientist or student in these things he may be, is able to explain how the object which is material becomes a matter of consciousness, which is spiritual.

Ralph Waldo Emerson, one of the most intuitional of men, who seems to sense a truth and then embody it in living language so pleasant to remember that it makes his every thought a treasure, said: "It is so wonderful to our neurologists that a man should see without eyes; but it does not occur to them that it is just as wonderful that he should see with them." Simple as the quoted fact seems, it is both wonderful and inexplicable that with eyes we should be able to see and make material objects manifest to our spirits.

It is not our purpose to write an essay on perception, which I seem to be doing, but only to philosophize a little in this way to smooth the abruptness of the statement, that our spirit friends do not see us objectively or materially in the sense that we mortals see each other. It is, however, no difficult thing for any or all spirits to see in this objective or external way, if they so desire, or for any purpose. It must be remembered that we are spirits now as well as materialized beings, and probably we are as well known in our spiritual aspects, by our friends in the spirit world, as we are ourselves by the memory or sight of us as encased in the mortal form.

I said it required material organs to see material things; they are easily found by spirits; the world is full of them. All the time there is a billion and almost a half at the service of the spirits. Spirits have only to come *en rapport* with the possessor of material optics or auricular ones in place, to thus see the world of nature or materiality as we mortals see it. So easy and so general is this that the spirits, through mediums, will often say they see us as we see each other; but I am sure for them to do so, which is very common, they do it in the way suggested, which is one slight remove from the direct objective way. The spirit has only to be conscious of the consciousness of the person by whose aid or with whose organs the said spirit sees to see objects as he does.

In one sense, as I have said, the object in normal human seeing is a foreign thing to the seer,—a discrete separation. for spirits cannot see, hear, or touch matter; only the image or sensation of it reaches the human sensorium. For instance, illustrating the point from an optical point of view, the image or picture of an object reaches the retina and is pictured on it, and that image or picture reaches the consciousness of the person who is looking at it: then it may be said to be the pictorial property of the spirit, and may be by the same source the property or consciousness of the spirit that is then *en rapport.* Some consideration of this point, which is really a matter strictly in the domain of science, is important in grasping the subject of the spiritual manifestations, or the dynamics of this more or less occult subject.

In corroboration of what has been said herein, I will quote from the writings of Eugene Crowell, where he writes on this subject, as follows: —

" It may here be proper to say something respecting the power of spirits to hear our conversation, as there are erroneous views prevalent even among Spiritualists upon this question. I have devoted considerable time and attention to this subject, and, as the result, I find that most spirits, unless on low planes, cannot distinctly hear us converse ; they more generally perceive our thoughts ; while, on the contrary, spirits on the lower planes cannot read our thoughts, but can more readily hear our conversation.

"Old John and Big Bear (two spirits) say their ability to hear mortal voices (when not in control) varies in every house they visit ? In my house they can understand our conversation best when a certain member of my family is present, and they elsewhere can hear best when some person present is mediumistic. In the presence of their medium they can always hear distinctly what is said by others. Through other reliable mediums, what is here stated has been confirmed, and it was only after thorough investigation that I accepted the assertion as hurtful, it being at variance with my preconceived opinions."

With the foregoing statement and quotation, the following experience will be illustrative and interesting, and will not only explain it, but will explain many of the utterances from the spirit world. One of the most reliable mediums I have ever known, and one who has given me demonstrative evidence of his genuine power, whose phase is the answering of sealed letters, and is entitled to his claim of keeping a spirit post-office. After receiving many answers through him from various spirits, one from my sister disturbed me. It was technically correct, and had never been opened, but it did not seem, in its extended answer to my query, to be the warm-hearted letter that my sister would have written: and if that was her now heavenly, platonic, dignified way, I felt that she must be so changed in the undress of the spirit that I had really lost my sister even if I had found her.

Seeking after the truth, and trying, as is my custom, to get at the facts of the case, I wrote a letter to my father, John Wetherbee, adding to the address inside, "or any of my spirit friends," asking four definite questions. My father was then alive, living in New York, but I wrote the letter as if it was for a spirit. I had sealed it up so that it could not be opened without my knowing it. I put no address on the envelope; that was entirely blank; no one but I knew for whom it was for.

I went with it to this medium, found him sitting

at his writing-table, took my seat opposite to him, and handed him the letter. He said he was tired, and so he would keep it till the next day, and laid it on the shelf with other letters. After a little general conversation upon other matters, as I knew him very well, he suddenly stopped, reached for the letter that he had placed on the shelf, and said the spirit was here, and he would answer it then. Please bear in mind that the letter had not been out of my sight. With the letter unaddressed and unopened before him, the fingers of his left hand resting on it, but not covering it, with his right hand he wrote, I looking on and reading as he wrote, as follows: " My dear son and namesake," and copied the questions literally in their order, and intelligently and elaborately answered each, as anyone could have done who had read the questions, and then he ended by saying, or rather writing: " Your once earthly but now spirit father, John Wetherbee."

The medium was very much surprised, when I opened and read the questions and name to him, that I was not satisfied. " What," said he, " do you expect?" I said: " The truth." My father was alive, and that lying spirit says: " Your once earthly and now spirit father." I was very much set back by this outcome, not understanding it then. One thing I was sure of, the perfect honesty of the medium, for I saw the production was honestly done before my eyes, only the spirit assumed to be my father when he was not. I soon got at the *rationale* of this, and lost my interest in such communications as identifications, but proved them to be spiritual beyond a doubt, and that was a great point settled, even if one was not sure who he was corresponding with.

The remarks I have made on seeing and hearing by the spirits explain how this mistake on the part of the spirits happened. Some spirits read the mind of the sitter. The spirits controlling the medium, his band as they call it, do the autographic work, reading probably clairvoyantly the letter which is unopened. They ought to be able to read the mind of the sitter or the writer of the letter. To do that, according to the ideas of Robert Dale Owen and Eugene Crowell, the executing spirit must be of a higher grade than the writer or sitter. It is hard to understand what higher or lower grade in spiritual parlance means, probably spiritually rather than intellectually; at any rate, it is on a different system from the expression "higher and lower" in this world's matters.

It was very evident the spirits on that occasion, besides not being my father or my departed friends, could not read my mind, which then and all the time was intensely charged with the thought. I was full of it, expecting some spirit would say: "You can reach your father by the mail terrestrial, but I will answer your questions." It almost seems, on the principle of mind-reading, that that might have been the result. Intense as the thought was in my mind, the spirits controlling this medium had no access to me, even if they had in a clairvoyant way to the sealed letter. I think, if I have been lucid in my statement, one will see where and how the mistake was made on the part of the spirits. The band controlling this medium, and friendly to him, did the work as best it could; not having access to my mind, they did not know my father was alive. I am glad they did not, for they then might have made a test of it for me when it would not have been one.

I have many times, since this paternal one, had sealed letters answered quite satisfactorily, and once or twice where the identity was quite complete,—at least I would be straining harder if I undertook to prove it a fiction than I would to consider it what it claimed to be. As I did not relate the circumstances of the letter or show its questionable genesis, but as an illustration of the subject treated, as well as to show the difficulties attending the identification of spirits generally, I will add in closing an account of one, that at least approximates to identification.

I had a reason for writing a letter to a certain spirit friend, to ask his opinion and advice, and, in the course of a few days I received an answer from that spirit, containing also the letter I had sent unopened. I put the missive in my pocket to read at leisure, and forgot all about it. On my way home, I stopped at Mrs. Mary Hardy's, the well-known medium, by appointment, and found a friend waiting there for me. We were going to have a sitting together. During the sitting, the spirit came that I had written to, and my friend said to the spirit: " Did you receive the letter that John wrote you the other day?" "Yes," said the spirit, "and I have answered it, and he has got it now in his pocket."

That reminded me of the fact which I had forgotten, and I said to my friend in his surprise: "That is so; I got it this morning and forgot all about it," and taking it out of my pocket, I said to him: "There it is." I do not see very easily how that could be anything else than a spirit's reply, and it seems to me it would be straining some not to admit it to have been actually, under the circumstances, from the very spirit to whom I had written. The clairvoyant eyes of the spirit could have seen possibly the message in my pocket, and thus got his information, but I am inclined to think it was from the identical spirit who knew the fact legitimately.

I have no question of the ability of reaching spirits and getting intelligent answers by writing in this way, but there is apt to be an uncertainty as to the identification, as was the case when I wrote to my living father in the form, as if he was a spirit, and got a reply from an *alias*, who assumed to be my "once earthly and now spirit father." I have pretty clear ideas how this is done, and why it is done by the spirits in the interest or benefit of the medium, and the fact of the work being done by spirits settles the important part of the question, for if one spirit can come, even a tricky one, so can a right and true one by the same law, if the conditions are right.

If that spirit who wrote the answer to me, assuming to be my once earthly father, had been Theodore Parker, or any high-toned spirit, on the principle suggested by Robert Dale Owen and Eugene Crowell, to whom I have referred, he could have read the strong desire already then formulated in my mind, and get the bottom facts in the case, and he would not have assumed to have been my father. I can conceive how such a spirit might have given me a perfect identification. I can conceive, also, how such a spirit might not have fancied my deception, and paid me in kind. That was the way the medium explained this affair. It was not satisfactory to me, for I know my motive was good, and that I was honestly seeking after truth. One can see there is great difficulty in knowing who the invisible really is that responds to you. It was a great pleasure to me to know beyond a question that the spirit was a bogus father, and to know, also, that the medium was honest clear through. It is a pleasure, also, to know that I have had some communications, of which I have spoken, through the same amanuensis that were in every way authentic.

The object of stating this point so minutely is for the guide of others,— for one to see there are disabilities to encounter, and not be unnecessarily suspicious of the medium, for the deficiencies may be farther in.

XXII.

A PENUMBRAL SKETCH.

*An afternoon with the spirits.—A departed friend
returns from over the river, and owns up.*

The following article I copy almost *verbatim* from
one I wrote and had published in the *Banner of
Light*. It embodies some interesting matters that
made a deep impression on me, as being unquestionably spiritual. The incidents that make the article
interesting to me come under the head of trifles in a
worldly sense, if anything is trifling that has the
luster of a spiritual source on it. I will, however,
present the article without much preface, letting it
speak for itself, which is as follows: —

> "Full oft my feelings make me start,
>   Like footprints on some desert shore,
> As if the chambers of my heart
>   Had heard their shadowy steps before."

I begin with these lines very much as we sing the
"Sweet By-and-Bye" at a seance, for the sake of the
proper conditions, and, at the same time, the weird
thought that the verse suggests expresses the state
of my mind at the present moment, having been

thinking of a late experience, and also while having the experience. It seems to be a proper state of mind in which to relate it. The experience was exceedingly interesting to me. Whether I can make it so to the reader remains to be seen.

Now, do not expect too much after this shadowy beginning, and thus be disappointed, but remember that sometimes the simplicities are in order, and very often with me, and, doubtless, with many others, some trifling incident among the manifestations will answer the earnest, hungry call in the following lines affirmatively (it is necessary to print them in this article, though quoted before in one of the chapters of this book, as the reader will see) when some wonderful manifestation might not, — the waters of Jordan, you remember, cured the royal leper when the larger rivers of his own country would not.

> "Ah, blow me the scent of one lily to tell
> That it grew outside of the world at most;
> Ah, show me a plume to touch, or a shell,
> That whispers of some unearthly coast."

Two of my friends from Providence called on me the other afternoon. One of them was a Spiritualist in a mild, quiet way, not conspicuously identified with the subject, but was a very firm believer, — had had evidences of its basic truth in his own home. The other was a legal gentleman of some repute, not a Spiritualist, I was going to say, but it is hard to tell who is and who is not, this thought has so penetrated the general mind. It seems he had been at some sittings at some earlier date, and thought there was something in it besides delusion and humbuggery, but had never been at a spiritual meeting; so neither was known in the city.

These two men, whom I will call Daniel and Ezekiel, because these two names popped into my mind, though in no sense suggestive of my friends, who are neither prophets, or the sons of prophets, both being men of the world, and of business.

"Well," said they, after the civilities were over, "what is there going on this afternoon? Where can we go and see something?"—meaning spiritual manifestations. We looked over the list; there were five or six interesting chances, but we could take in but one, and as there was not much time before they would begin, and, possibly, then the one selected would be full; but, like Luath, the dog of which Burns speaks,—

"His honest, sonsie, baws'nt face,
Aye gat him friends in ilka place."

So they had no fears on that score, but took their chances, and went to see the "Berry sisters," who are materializing mediums, as well as for other physical manifestations, and we moved in their direction. Though it did not happen to be a materialization seance, when we got there, as we expected, it was one of the occasions when none of us were disappointed.

As I have said, Daniel and Ezekiel were entire strangers to the medium, and were not introduced for obvious reasons, and they were unknown also to all the persons present. This happened to be Miss Ellen Berry's dark circle. Daniel did not seem to get much during this seance (some people somehow always seem to get more than others). With Ezekiel it was otherwise. The medium, who was seated at some distance from the latter (Daniel sitting at one end of a twelve-foot table, and Ezekiel side of me at the other end), she being seated about in the center, said she heard the name of Ezekiel H——; that was the full name of my friend; and later, when the medium was sitting nearer to him, the same name came, and also one or two of his relatives' names were mentioned; they also wrote some messages. They were from two or three different spirits, and were remarkably good tests. I was presuming Ezekiel H—— was the name of my friend, but it seems it was an uncle of the same name, and the message showed the fact, besides his information in reply to a question from me, as I did not know he had an uncle who was a namesake.

I always am interested in tests; but I generally have to get them by observation, as in this case, for personally my spirit friends are apt to be known to the mediums, for my pen is such a tell-tale. On this occasion, however, I not only realized my friend's tests, which were unmistakably so to him, and therefore to me, but I had them directly, also, and this is what I referred to when I began this article. It is unnecessary to speak of Albert and Hattie, or the spirits of Amory and Huntington, who manifested to me for reasons mentioned; they would hardly be tests; and yet in Hattie's manifestation there was something worth mentioning. She kissed me on the forehead and whispered her name, and in doing so she was so near I felt her hair as it touched my head and face, and the medium being seated closely by my side, and I holding her hand, I know she did not and could not move, and the circle being unbroken I know that it was some unearthly head and hair that whispered and came in contact with mine; and I hope the writer of that verse who wanted a shell "that whispered of some unearthly coast," or anybody else who is hungry in that direction, will take my word that if an " unearthly head " will answer as well as a "shell," or "the scent of a lily," that it has been my experience. I seem to be spinning this out; but I have not yet reached the circumstance that has inspired my pen.

My friend, Seth E. Brown,— I will be excused in using names, I am sure he will not object to it, and I am something like Junius, who wrote the letters, who liked to deal with persons, not with shadows; yet I am not like him, for I do and am dealing with "shadows" in this book; but now, in dealing with Brown, I am dealing with a person who now may pass for a "shadow." But it pleases me to feel that the most substantial things in the universe are spirits; they are the real, we are the fleeting. "We," as Emerson says, "are only the flux of matter over the wires of thought."

My friend Brown died very suddenly about five or six weeks ago (May, 1884), and who until a year ago

was a joint tenant with me in the business office I
occupied, and we had been together in this way for
several years. We were very intimate in a business
way, and many an hour have we chatted on these
spiritual matters. He was not a Spiritualist, but
was very hospitable to the subject; probably like many
others he believed more than he had the courage to
admit. He thought I had had great evidence, and
wished that he had. He often said: "We will all
know some day whether it is true;" in fact, after any
long colloquy on the subject, that was his stereotyped
ending,—meaning by it that when we died we should
know then whether we were still alive. He generally
said, also, or did sometimes, that if he died before I
did he would come and let me know if it was true.
"So do," I replied, and said ditto. It was not many
weeks before he died that I had one of these chats
with him, which was ended with that usual remark.

While at this seance of which I have been speaking, with Daniel and Ezekiel, and during the manifestations that were then going on, I had some very
vigorous pounds on the top of my head, and I said
mentally, as that was the usual way, "Is that——?"
(mentioning the name of a spirit friend, but not
speaking it vocally), and got one smart touch by the
spirit on my head which means "No" as the response.
I continued then in the same way to ask the names
of my departed friends, and the response was "No"
every time, and then Brown's name popped into my
mind, and almost before I got it mentally formulated,
as if the spirit knew it as quickly as I did, the "Yes"

came quite vigorously, and I said: "Is that really you, Seth?" only I did not say "Seth" vocally, but thought it. Besides the three pounds on my head, I got quite a number on my back, and I have no doubt it was the spirit of my friend. It was almost as if he had said: "Did I not tell you, John, that I would come?"

The medium later, and sitting at another part of the table farther from me, said, addressing me: "That friend of yours is still with you; he seems very glad; his name is Seth, I cannot get the rest of his name." That was right, but the medium did not know it, for his name had not then been mentioned. I had been very particular. When the room was lighted again, I found I had some messages written by the spirits the same way that my friend Ezekiel had, of which I have spoken. I will mention here that when the messages were written to me and to Ezekiel, I held the medium's hand, and know that she did not do the writing, and with that company it is absurd to talk of confederates. I am cutting this short, and leaving out many of the points of this seance for the sake of brevity, and confine myself as much as possible to the Brown complexion of this experience.

Among the messages from Albert, Hattie, and others was this one from Brown: "*John, I believe it now.—Seth.*" This was a very short message; but it seemed very appropriate, and what I ought to have expected from him, if it was he. The medium never knew Mr. Brown, or my connection with him. I was not expecting him nor thinking of him, and I began to exhaust the names of my departed friends when his name occurred to me. I really think it was he, and his message though short was full of meaning,— *multum in parvo*,— " I believe it now." It certainly made an intelligent connection with our antecedent talks to which I have referred, and wholly unknown to the medium and anyone else in the room but me.

At the close of this seance my friends, as well as myself, felt as if the two hours we had spent with Miss Berry as being the " gates ajar," and among the departed, had not been time wasted. We all three talked over the matter by ourselves. Ezekiel had oral and other tests, and many remarkable messages, which were what might have been expected from the spirits communicating. One message from a distinguished, but departed, lawyer of his city was very satisfactory. I knew the man by reputation, but did not know him as in any way connected with Ezekiel, but it seems he was on quite intimate terms, and the message was in keeping with it, and he went home pretty strong in the faith. In fact, we all three can be counted on as Spiritualists, if there were any doubts before.

I began this penumbral sketch with a verse of poetry, and perhaps it will be as well for symmetry to end with one. I sometimes think a verse, with a sublime and fitting thought in it, is more suggestive and ornamental than a peroration, so I draft on the following : —

" I feel their touch upon my hair,
     Upon my cheek and on my brow;
I know that they are everywhere,
     That they are with me even now."

XXIII.

MATERIALIZATION.

Affirmations. — Critical comments. — Illustrative Experiences.

I will begin a chapter on this subject by saying the materialization of human forms, or what is called by that name, is a fact, — that is, human forms are produced, extemporized so to speak, into visible, tangible, or sensuous apparitions. I firmly believe this, both theoretically and practically, — have had the evidence that makes me sure of what I so positively state.

Speaking of it theoretically, I have had, as the reader of this book will know, in my own house, and under the most favorable conditions, sensuous, tangible, and intelligent evidence of the materialization of a seemingly human hand that I could grasp, and have had that evidence hundreds of times. I have had also the handling and close ocular inspection of hands of apparent flesh and bones, in fact, real human hands, that were not attached to human bodies, but were as alive and pliable and sensitive as my own. Now, therefore, giving us a hand materialized, the production of the whole form is possible also. These experiences of mine were long before the advent of the full-form manifestations; this, then, is my ground for believing in the phase theoretically.

I have had experience with about all of the mediums for materialization who have been in this vicinity, and have had some ocular proof that these forms are, sometimes at least, what they claim to be; not to the extent I wish, but added to the fact that, with the majority of mediums for this phase, I have had perfect proof that personating, acting a part, or confederacy, is not the *modus operandi* of their production. This, then, is my ground for believing in the phase practically.

I must, also, with my experience, add that, to me, as a whole, it is not the most interesting phase of the spiritual phenomena. I can say, with Leigh Hunt: —

> " How sweet it were if, without feeble fright,
> Or dying of the dreadful beauteous sight,
> An angel came to us, and we could bear
> To see it issue from the silent air
> At evening in our room —"

because the evidence through the sense of sight, as an eminent *savant* has said, is stronger testimony than evidence through the senses of hearing and touch. I am hardly prepared to admit that, it depends so much on what we are testing, and our intellectual make-up, as connected with our several senses. But, referring to the poetic suggestion, the manifestations of spirit forms have never come "at evening in our room " in a way that would respond to Leigh Hunt's "sweet" possibility, as suggested by the quotation, and, in fact, has been the dream or fancy, bordering almost upon expectation of the poets generally, as memory and records will show. So, as I have said, believing in the fact both theoretically and practically, I am not fascinated with the materialized return of departed spirits as I would be if they came in a less questionable manner. I hardly know how to express what I want to say; but I trust in the elaboration of my thought I will make my ideas manifest and manifestly friendly to the phase, before I get through the chapter.

In spiritual manifestations, as in scientific research, we must make the most of the best conditions we can get. One cannot always command his conditions, whether spiritual or scientific. We are obliged in astronomy to look at the sun or stars through forty miles or more of atmosphere; it is possible, if we could command an independent standpoint, we might have to modify some of our conclusions. Now, it seems darkness is a requisite condition for the production of materialized spirit forms; not total darkness, but a very few degrees above it, and that, certainly, is one of the disabilities, especially in this particular phase, as recognition is the attractive point; and, therefore, the spirits may as well not come for that purpose, unless there can be light enough to be unmistakable. I am not finding any fault, for I am only too glad for their apparition any way.

I am very hospitable to the spiritual manifestations generally, especially to materializations, hoping the latter will improve, as they have, to a great degree, already, and that I yet may be as fascinated with them as I am with many of the simpler, yet intelligent, phenomena; but all this wishing and hoping need not prevent the expression of my thoughts or views on the subject, even as it appears to me, and to say, though in one instance, I can say I recognized a spirit, and this fact of a positive recognition threw a luster on the phase generally, by making it possible that some others that I ought have, but could not recognize, may have been the persons they claimed to be. As the remembrance of that satisfactory one, with its accompanying luster, recedes into the distant past, I sometimes wonder myself if it was really so, and I seem to need repetitions to keep me firm in the rut of that one special experience.

As I read my recorded story of it now, which I know I wrote truthfully, and as I felt the reading of it, and the memory of it, among so many less impressively true ones since, have detracted some of the vividness of that one, and I find myself asking in my own mind if that was really so, paled a little, like a neglected photograph taken years ago, and yet from my habits of making records I know it was so.

Now for illustration of the subject generally. I can remember very distinctly my dark-eyed sister. I can remember her as plainly as if she now sat before me; and if she should appear at one of these seances as plainly as I now see her in my mind, how readily I could recognize her. But this spirit has never appeared so; she has come, so the form has said, but in such questionable shape I never could have known her; and, if she is around me now, she knows I could not recognize a young woman of dark curly hair, and large, bright, black eyes, dressed flowingly in white, her head-dress flowing, and white, also, not a speck of dark hair in sight, and no speculation in her eye. These phantasms — no, not phantasms, they are too human and muscular for that — do not attract me as the actual presence of my spirit friends, or even as being the personal presence of spirits. This was my experience in ocular recognitions until my friend Albert appeared, and it was so like him, though almost speechless, with his manifest, quiet manner, the whole phase rose higher in my estimation, and I have the faith that it will go on improving, and these disabilities grow less and less.

It seemed to me, before the time of which I am speaking, and so it has since that in observing others' recognitions, that they came to their conclusions quicker than I could. It is possible there is a difference in people's eyes, some seeing better in the dark than others. I have sometimes wondered if people had not intuitive help, perhaps some clairvoyant power supplementing the ocular. I am only making these observations to show the state of my own mind, not for any special information or instruction, or I would write an essay on the subject, which this certainly is not.

The most interesting feature to me in these materi-

alizations, and which I consider spiritual manifestations, is not in the personalities of the apparitions, but
in the fact that they are spirit manifestations. When
I have satisfied myself that a woman, passing from
us and going behind a curtain into the triangular
space in the corner of a room, and the woman by
measurement is under five feet in stature, and there
is no way for a confederate to go into that enclosure
without my seeing him or her enter, and then there
comes out of that triangular space into the room a
man six feet high, and I shake hands with him, and
know he is alive and not on stilts, but standing or
walking firmly and naturally on the floor, I know
then there is no possible metamorphosis from the
medium into that spirit. It is of no consequence
whether the apparition is John Brown or General
Burnside or my uncle,— that is not the point.

There is a human-looking form that I know is not
the medium, and is not a confederate, and being then
an extemporized one it must be spiritual, because it
is an intelligent act, and an intelligent apparition,
and there is no intelligence that is not connected
with either a mortal or a spirit. That, then, of itself
is an interesting fact, and a wonderful one. If this
fact or apparition claims to be some departed friend
of mine, that I would know if I saw him or her, and
yet do not know the apparition, that does not add to
the interest of the manifestation; it detracts, if anything. The spirit had better remain a "beauty and
a mystery" than assume to be some special personal
friend that is unrecognizable.

I cannot think of a departed friend, male or female. that I could not recognize in a light even below the reading point, if they came looking as they did when I knew them or last saw them. If they are in any disguise by unusual drapery or growth, so that we can only take their word for it, having necessarily our doubts, and deficient as they all are in loquacity or fluency or loudness of speech, they might as well remain *incog*. The interest centering in form manifestations at present to me is much more in the fact than in the recognitions. I make a great distinction between intellectual and optical recognitions, and I shall say a word further on that distinction.

Now I will relate a few experiences of the many I have had that have interested me. I will begin with this one. I went into a cabinet at the commencement of a seance with the medium, at her request. She was clothed as ordinarily in a dark slate-colored dress. She sat in a chair facing the opening, and quite near as it was a shallow one. I stood front of her, back to the opening, holding each of her hands in one of mine. There was a purpose in it as the reader will see. When she said "That will do," I then dropped her hands, and turned to go out. I did not move a step forward as the cabinet was shallow, as I have said; but parting the curtain I was visible to persons in the circle who began to notice me, holding up their hands or saying: "See, see it!" I thought to myself they were taking me for a spirit. On turning a little I saw what they had noticed; it was a female spirit close behind me clothed in white, arms extended;

the spirit was taller than I was, as I had to look up a little at her face, while the medium was shorter.

The principal thing to notice here was the impossibility for a woman, dressed darkly, sitting in a chair whose contiguity I had not left, to appear instantly as a taller person, clothed in white. I am as sure there were, on this occasion, two personalities — the medium and the spirit, and no confederate assistance — as I am that I am now writing on paper. I may be different from many others, but how comparatively insignificant is the more or less doubtful recognition of some departed friend by the side of this perfect evidence of an extemporized human form?

On one occasion, when attending a very satisfactory seance, where the cabinet was a curtained, shallow alcove, with no entrance to it but from the room where we were sitting, and in sight of us, I am as positive there was but one person in the inclosure — that being the medium — as I am that earth is attended with but one moon. Many recognitions were made of the spirits appearing from time to time by some of the persons in the circle; they were not very convincing to me as recognitions, but that was no concern of mine. The fact of their being apparitions at all is what interested me, and of that I have no doubt. At last, a female spirit appeared at the parted curtain, and signified by a nod, after parties had severally said "Is it for me?" that it was for me, and I went up to the cabinet. I presumed it or her to be one of my friends that I could not recog-

nize. As usual, this form was voiceless. I felt that
if I had said : "Is it Hannah or Emeline or Adeline?"
she would have nodded affirmatively, but I asked no
such leading question. I said in a hospitable voice
that I was glad to see her, whoever she was; hoped
she was well and happy, and having a good time
generally; to which she, in her mute way, assented.
I shook hands with her, and got such a good, solid
grip of an apparently muscular hand that, in my
mind, I concluded to keep it, and did so, by no
means to pull her out into exhibition, but simply
"to hold the fort."

In a second or two the spirit, as might have been
expected, intimated a withdrawal of her hand, and
I advanced closer, saying : "Do you want me to
enter?" She signified "Yes," and I went into the
pitch-dark enclosure, her hand firmly in mine, I having, as I said, a good grip with my right hand. With
my left hand I felt of the medium, who was sitting
down, so I had perfect evidence it was not a dummy,
but the medium, I still holding the hand of the
spirit. When conscious of there being two presences, I found nothing in my hand, only my closed
hand which had never relaxed; the spirit hand that
I had held was not withdrawn ; it had dissolved into
nothing,—dematerialized, as it is called,—and I had,
as I have said, an empty hand. The medium, at
that point, came out of the trance. I parted the
curtain, and we two came out into the room.

I am sure, so were all, that a few moments before
there were three presences in that cabinet,— the

spirit, the medium, and this scribe; there were now only two,— the extemporized form, apparently as human and substantial as the remaining two, had dissolved again into the invisible air. This, then, is an evidence of the production of a form, visible and tangible to the senses; to me it is incomparably a more satisfactory evidence than what have been recognitions in my presence, because the fact itself is demonstrated. The impression that I am trying to give in this dissertation is that the value of the fact is of more consequence than any claimed personality, whether historical characters or from our several tribal or social circles.

From what I have seen, and am sure of, in this department of Spiritualism, I have faith that it will continue to improve. I see already a difference in the conditions on different occasions in the make-up of the circle, affecting the quality of the manifestations and the degree of light permitted. I have been in carefully-selected circles where the presentations or productions were great improvements, even by the same medium, over those in the presence of promiscuous gatherings. I am not without faith that this phase of the phenomena has come to stay, and to improve; and the apparitions improve; and, exhibited under a brighter light, the recognitions will be more apparently genuine and unmistakaable; for, say what you will, these forms, as a general thing, are rather stupid-looking; they lack brightness and intelligence much more than they do muscular and physical vigor.

I have said but little about frauds. I am not
unmindful of them, and their liability. The conditions of darkness, cabinets, side rooms, and credulity
permit them. I am presuming, however, that the
reader will understand that I have been open-eyed in
all directions, and when I speak as positively as I
do, and have done in these several "shadows," it
will be understood that I have taken into consideration the many disabilities connected with, at least,
this phase of the manifestations. It seems hardly
worth while for me to write out the details of detec-
tion; the reader must presume I am not a fool, and
if he cannot presume so, what I say any way will be
of no account, and I am not writing for his benefit.

There is no question that there are disadvantages
enough in this phase of the materialization of forms
to make it peculiarly liable to fraud, notwithstanding
the sacredness of the subject, particularly in its commercial or business aspect. There are frauds, also,
where the medium is not to blame; it may be on the
part of the spirits, and in the fine magnetic lines of
attractive and repulsive influences; the audience
may be, and unquestionably is, a factor in the manifestation, both in drawing around like-minded spirits,
and also in furnishing "raw material," so to speak,
to help in the materialization.

It is no use, however, to excuse the medium for
the overt act if caught personating a spirit, or with
the paraphernalia of decoration; she must take the
consequences, whether audiences or spirits are to
blame or not, though it is possible for such an act to

be perpetrated, and the medium to be perfectly innocent. I never make this as an argument to anyone.
I would expect to be laughed at if I did; but those
who know something of the dynamics of this subject
know I am right.

I can hardly understand the motive on the part of
spirits for deception; the fact, however, is unquestionable. I have known the personation of a spirit
by the medium, where the latter was innocent and
wholly unconscious, and the form was allowed by
the spirit controlling to be accepted as a materialization. I think a fraud out of order always, whether
by spirit or mortal. A transfiguration is as wonderful a manifestation as a materialization. Why the
spirits permit a form of that kind to come forward
and be received as an extemporized presence, or a
materialization, is very strange, to say the least, and
I think the less of them for it. I feel myself that,
when I am a spirit, if I should be attracted to this
business of extemporizing forms, which is very doubtful, they would be what they claimed to be, or there
would be no apparitions.

I think I have now said about enough, if I have
been lucid, for anyone who cares to know where to
place me, which is as a firm believer in the fact of
materialization with the same difficulty of identification as in the other phases of the manifestations, and
that the fact of identification in all phases of the
manifestations is a subordinate one to the main issue,
which is of answering Job's question affirmatively,—
"If a man die, shall he live again?"

If the "Sage of Galveston" were alive, he would ay here is a good place to stop. Why should I say "if alive," when the chapter on his return proves him so? Well, it is only a figure of speech. The "Sage" thought, however, may have been a whisper, and if this were a newspaper article here would have been my period in response. Writing now in a more permanent form, I will say to my invisible friend that I think I had better add an affirmative illustration or two just for a finish, and will do so.

A daughter of mine, whom the reader will remember as Hattie, has come to me in materialized form several times. Of course I could not recognize a lady of thirty who passed out of sight a child of six. This spirit once came, called me "Father," and gave her name as "Hattie," softly but audibly. She made a sign with her hands, indicating her light when she died, or when I last saw her; this certainly was pretty good evidence. A few days after I was accidentally at a sitting with a test medium, who did not know that I had been at a materialization, and Hattie came through or controlled her; said she showed herself to me at the dark circle the other evening. Both experiences made what I would call an intellectual recognition, and the fact was a very interesting one.

Some year or two after that, and not very long ago, she came again; this time Miss Berry was the medium. As I sat in the circle, the lady sitting next to me, whom I did not know, but who was a medium, said to me: "Have you a Hattie, a young lady in the spirit world?" I said "Yes." "She is your daughter, is she not?" "Yes," said I; then she said: "She has been standing by you, and leaning on you all the evening."

In about half an hour after that, the lady not having moved or spoken to anyone, so this episode was private, the manager of the circle said: "Hattie Wetherbee is here, and says she will try to show herself to her father." I went up to the cabinet, and very soon the spirit of a young lady appeared and embraced me, and retired. I say spirit because that is the custom; but these forms have more of a material than a spiritual aspect, all of them; hence I suppose the designation, materialization. In a little while she opened the curtain again, and, putting her head close to mine, whispered to me saying: "Father, I have been with you all the evening," pointing to my seat, and adding: "You knew it, too, for I got her to tell you." I think this, also, was a circumstantial or intellectual recognition, and I consider it an interesting circumstance. I will add, however, that the two "forms" of what claimed to be Hattie at those two different times were very far from being duplicates. They were not out of keeping, however, to what my daughter might have been at her maturity; but one was six or eight inches taller, and every way larger than the other, so that dissimilarity is a drawback to identification, unless spirit forms are elastic, which is not unsupposable; but as spiritual manifestations, with the circumstances, it seems to me they were perfect.

One more circumstance I think will be all that

"the invisible Sage" will allow me to add to this chapter. This was a very interesting occasion, and also was at the Berry sisters'. The circle was select and special, small and for a purpose. I will not give a full description of it; I will copy from my record book the circumstance that specially interested me. Among the forms that appeared was the apparition of a relative. I did not recognize her, so I asked her name. The spirit replied: "I am Mary Smith."

Mary Smith was my mother's cousin, who had been dead forty years, and was a maiden lady of sixty when she passed away. I remember her as she looked then as well as I remember my mother. She appeared on this occasion as "a radiant maiden" well preserved of middle life, yet she was then a century old. That somewhat contradicted the poet's affirmation where he says:—

> "Little of all we value here,
> Wakes on the morn of its hundredth year,
> Without both looking and feeling queer."

Not so contradictory however upon a second reading. She looked, as we trust all old people do, in the spirit world,—a sort of youthful maturity.

Of course, I could not see anything in this fine-looking, well-arrayed person to remind me of cousin Mary. In her life, she was an educated lady of refinement. Her sister was the wife of the venerable poet, Richard H. Dana, who died, aged ninety, a few years ago. I mention this to show that her social surroundings were of a high order, and it may have had something to do with her rather extra-radiance on this occasion, so that I was rather proud to renew her acquaintance and relationship in her well-preserved condition. For fear the reader will think I am straining to hold on to this relationship, I will say that after announcing her name in a small, sweet, low-toned, but distinct voice, she said: "Adeline and Hattie are here with me, and so is Albert," and a little more that need not be repeated. No one present knew the relative connection of these names and circumstances, which seem to have been added for the sake of identification, and that gave me another tolerably good intellectual recognition. Well, I think I had better stop here, even if abruptly, and to take the edge off of such may be *Sage* abruptness, I will add the following poetic thought, or semi-information : —

> "Ghosts of happy, fond illusions,
>   Flitting over land and sea,
> Through my heart your viewless footsteps
>   Come and go eternally."

XXIV.

CUI BONO?

What is the good of it all, even admitting it to be true?
—The answer self-evident.

Cui bono,— what is the good of it? some say; and
it is generally by worldly and unthinking people,
and, perhaps, after listening to testimony that they
cannot deny or explain. It is a question I rarely
answer. It does not seem to me worthy of an
answer. If the answer to it is not at once self-evident to the questioner to answer it, or by argument
to make it appear of value, seems to me like casting
pearls before swine. The remark of James Russell
Lowell seems to be applicable, where he says: "The
only way to argue with an east wind is to put on
your overcoat."

When that thoughtful, scholarly writer, Ernest
Renan says: "If we could each of us be sure, once a
year, of exchanging two words only with the loved
and lost, death would be no more death," he stated
a truth, and I do not think anyone will doubt it. Is
not, then, that silly or thoughtless question answered?
When Henry Thomas Buckle, that profound student,

and who was not one of the believers in a future life, or, more properly, was an agnostic in his views of the matter, said that, "If mankind was deprived of its belief in immortality, lean and unsatisfactory as it is, it would be insane from despair," did he not answer the *cui bono?* Is not, then, the sensuous proof of a life beyond the grave, of itself, a boon to mankind? Both of these affirmations show that the human heart is hungry for this light.

Is there not a reply to the question *cui bono?* in food for the hungry, and is it not as essential or important to feed the spirit of a man as to feed his body? One who spoke with authority said: "Man cannot live by bread alone." Anyone who says *cui bono?* at what Spiritualism proposes, or what it practically is, says in plain language that man can live by bread alone, and there are many that do live so, and, verily, they will have their reward.

If the man says *cui bono?* because he knows there is no future life beyond this, or that it appears so to him, and that we are knocking where there is no door, then it is a waste of time, and *cui bono?* is the proper question to ask; but that has no bearing on the subject. Modern Spiritualism makes a positive statement. It says there are intelligent phenomena that claim to be the voice of the departed; and when it cannot be denied or accounted for by the party, and he says *cui bono?* the question is an absurd one, for if there is no such future, of course there is no good to come from it. The asking of the question, then, is begging it negatively.

Modern Spiritualism, in its basic fact, is either true or it is false. If true, as we have said, the bare fact answers the question of *cui bono?* If it is false, the question is superfluous.

There is something in human life that is of essential value besides " bread and butter," — that is, besides health, wealth, popularity, or position. Prof. Tyndall deals with values, and in a scientific manner. He says: " The circle of human nature, then, is not complete without the arc of feeling and emotion. The lilies of the field have a value for us beyond their botanical ones, — a certain lightening of the heart accompanies the declaration that 'Solomon in all his glory was not arrayed like one of these.' The sound of the village bell which comes mellowed from the valley to the traveler upon the hill has a value beyond its acoustical one. The starry heavens, as you know, had for Immanuel Kant a value beyond their astronomical one. Round about the intellect sweeps the horizon of the emotions from which all our noblest impulses are derived. I think it very desirable to keep this horizon open; not to permit either priest or philosopher to draw down his shutters between you and it."

Anyone who asks the question : "What is the good of it?" in reference to the claim of modern Spiritualism, has his shutters so thoroughly drawn down that he does not know what light is; he is an eyeless fish in the Mammoth Cave of materialism.

The editor of the *Scientific American*, who does not believe at all in modern Spiritualism, but, on the

contrary opposes it, does not say *cui bono?* he pays
this tribute to it, with an "if." "If it be true," he
says, "such words as vast, profound, tremendous
would have to be strengthened a thousand-fold to be
fitted to express its importance. If true, it will
become the one great event in the world's history.
It will give an imperishable luster of glory to the
nineteenth century." These are my sentiments also,
without any "if."

Here we all are in this world, faith gone into eclipse,
revelation weakening in its foundations, the intuitions of the soul following faith into its eclipse,
because the records of holy writ do not rest on the
bed rock,—doubt and agnosticism intruding into the
human mind. Now comes some intelligent phenomena into the world of human thought that, if
true, throws a luster of truth on the ancient records,
or at least proves a spiritual source for what is called
revelation, and reproduces the fore-world of confidence again; and, if it does so, who asks the question,
cui bono? — certainly no one but a thoughtless igno-
ramus.

Epes Sargent, speaking of matters bearing on this
point, says: "This universe, you may be sure, is not
an infinite contrivance for the production and swift
extinction of sentient, loving, intelligent life. It is
not a stupendous vestibule to a charnel house, where
affection, friendship, science, and art find congenial
and progressive recipients for a few fleeting moments,
and man is admitted to a glimpse of a possible happiness and growth, and then plunged into the black-

ness of annihilation, — a world where life and mind are given only to be withdrawn, as if in mockery, and truth and goodness are as evanescent as falsehood and evil."

Is not the "fact" an important one, if it settles affirmatively that death and the grave is not the end of a man's life; that the man survives death, and has a continued or perpetual conscious life beyond it? Does anyone question the value or *cui bono?* of that fact because, in his estimation, it is not yet proved or provable? It does not alter the fact of the claim that it makes. Can anything be conceived that is of more value to the people of this world, and more conducive to their well-being and moral worth than to know beyond a peradventure that our fathers, mothers, brothers, sisters, friends, who are the lost stars in our several social circles, are still alive, conscious of our in-comings and our out-goings, and, as of old, having a real though invisible supervision over us? If anyone does not see the matter in this light, then *cui bono?* is their proper query, to which I make no reply except to say, in the language of Scripture, that I have no pearls to cast away.

XXV.

Containing some thoughts on prophecy, critical and illustrative.

The following article was written for and printed in a magazine; the inspiring motive was the words: "Will he enlighten us?" Some one, somewhere, had criticised me on my ideas on the subject of prophecy. The only memorandum I have now to refresh my memory reads thus: "Why should Brother Wether- bee not hope for the time to come when a more intelligent method obtains of forecasting future events? He sees wisdom in our ignorance of events to occur in the future; we do not. Will he enlighten us?" This memorandum does not bring into my mind the circumstances that called for this question, and led me to write the article referred to. Reading it over lately, I thought it, or at least some of it, was worth preservation; so, it being short, I will copy it, as follows: —

As the four words, "Will he enlighten us?" linger in my mind as an inspiring impulse, the lines of Emerson arise in my memory. It is an orphic but

characteristic expression of a rather weird flavor.
There is no remarkable definiteness in the thought,
and yet it seems to carry a suggestive undertone
which hints at a connection between prevision and
"the thing so signified." I hardly think any words
of mine will bring the poet's idea into more bold
relief, and the best thing I can do is to quote it, and
then leave it : —

> "Delicate omens traced in air
> To the lone bard true witness bear;
> Birds with auguries on their wings
> Chanted undeceiving things
> Him to beckon, him to warn;
> Well might then the poet scorn
> To learn of scribe or courier
> Hints writ in vaster character;
> And on his mind, at dawn of day,
> Soft shadows of the evening lay;
> For the prevision is allied
> Unto the thing so signified :
> Or say, the foresight that awaits
> Is the same genius that creates."

The simple presentation of these lines will serve
the purpose of concentrating my thought, and I hope
they will the reader's also ; if not, read the quotation slowly and thoughtfully over again ; it will bear
study.

It is possible the time may come when the pedes-
tal of prophecy will be a firm and reliable one, when
prevision may become an exact science like astronomy, a matter of mathematics to which I added in
my communication, " I hope not; I have no welcome
for it." I still think there is wisdom in letting

future suns shine on future days without anticipat-
ing future sunshine or cloud by any system of discount. Still, I have a hospitable, or open eye, for
truth and knowledge. I follow wherever truth leads.
I presume I have the same feeling regarding the subject of prevision, should it become a matter of scientific or mathematical exactness, like the calculation
of an eclipse, or the transit of a planet across the
sun's disk, that, perhaps, Jesus may have had when
he said: "Father, let this cup pass from me; nevertheless, not my will but thine be done," feeling sure
it will be done any way.

Quoting this remark from the Bible leads me to
think that Jesus may have been a mind-reader as
well as intuitive and prophetic, and, perhaps, sensed
the future feeling in this way; he may, perhaps, have
sensed the collective and unspoken thought or sentiment of the multitude, and may thus have known
something of his painful and mortifying exit, or that
it was to be inevitable, and so said to himself in his
grief: "I hope not; I have no desire for it;" or,
what amounts to the same thing,— the letter of the
record,— "let this cup pass from me."

A distinguished doctor and scientific man said in
my hearing once that "If mankind knew each one
the date when their own individual life was to end,
— that is, his exit, as definite in the future as the
coming of one's birthday, or of Christmas,— more
than half of mankind would go crazy." It was the
matter of death that I had in my mind in what I said
in the article to which I referred. Hence the knowl-

edge would not be wisdom, even if it should ever be truth. It seems to me the spirit world sees it in that light; and though I do not think it has established itself very solidly on its prophetic power, but seeing a disposition on the part of mortals who believe in spirit messages to place some confidence in their predictions, the spirits hesitate in expressing their opinion on the mortuary point.

Renan, who wrote the "Life of Christ," who had some belief in the conscious existence of the departed, said: "If each of us could once a year be permitted to exchange but two words with the loved and the lost, death would be no more death" I find that the waves of new truth which are ever rolling in, and forever will be, come into current knowledge about the time the race is ready for them.

If what Renan, the French scholar says, is true, and what modern Spiritualism is beginning to make a fact, and is certainly softening down death's terrors from a grim messenger to an angelic one, the prevision of life's exit may not always be as unwelcome as it is now to the average of mankind. When it will not be the fact, as that doctor said, that half of mankind would go crazy if they knew as definitely to a day and hour their demise, as they know the day and hour of some coming birthday or anniversary, there may be such a change that people will rejoice at such a prevision, if the event was near, as they would to an appointment to some desirable foreign mission, or a promotion.

This will, perhaps, explain my remarks on the

possible future better or more scientific method than now obtains. I was and am speaking of the matter in the light of today, and, although I had human life mainly in my mind, the unwisdom of which I then spoke, applies to future events generally.

I think, however, there is a psychic power or intelligence of an emotional or intuitive character manifested even in the flux of human and current affairs that seems to sense the future. Occasionally that knowledge leaks into mundane minds definitely. It comes sometimes in such a detailed manner that we know it is not accidental, or coincident, or in any sense a guess, that it is actually a prevision (instances in proof of this fact will be found in some of the chapters of this book, so need not be repeated here).

Among many instances in proof of what I say, I will relate one. My mother's older sister, who died a spinster a few years ago at the age of 85, was a very singular woman,— very mediumistic, sensitive, and nervous. A history of her singularities would be quite illustrative of this subject, only her premonitions often lacked the dignity and sublimity that celestial influences ought to carry; but, letting all that rest, she came down stairs one morning in a very pensive state of mind,— noticeably so; but seemed disinclined to tell her grief.

She was at this time a woman of about half a century old, and in tolerably good health, as her length of life afterwards indicated. Being alone with her during a part of the day, and manifesting some curiosity, she explained her sadness. She said she had

had a singular dream. She was looking out of the
front window; and, instead of seeing Hancock Street,
as she ought to, she saw nothing but an extensive
grave-yard, stones, monuments, here and there and
everywhere. On some were dead people's names
written, and on some living people's names. Every
name she saw was a relative or an ancestor, or some
friend with whom she was acquainted.

The greater number of these names seemed to
be of those still living. On each stone, under the
name, was the year 1806, or 1820, or 1860, or 1875, or
whatever it might be (this dream occurred between
1830 and 1840; I think about 1833). She saw quite
distinctly twelve grave-stones in a row, with the
names of her eleven brothers and sisters, and her
own, on them, arranged in the order of their birth,
and the year of their death on each. This was the
conspicuous feature of this cemetery, which, when
observed, became a matter of interest, and the other
part of the dreamy tableau began to grow dim, and
recede, and soon formed no part of the picture, only
the twelve stones with her brothers' and sisters'
names remaining, and they seemed quite conspicuous
and near. Soon that part vanished, and she awoke,
but she was able to remember the years only of five
of them,— two brothers and a sister, who had died,
and two living sisters; and the two sisters did die in
the years that were on the stones named for them in
the dream.

The inference is that if she could have remembered
the years of death mentioned on the other seven

grave-stones, she would have had a prevision of the year of death of all the members of her family. For some wise purpose, the veil of forgetfulness was drawn over them. Certainly, in that dream there was proved that somehow or somewhere there is the principle of prophecy. With this, and other instances in my own, as well as the world's, history, it shows what is possible, and yet I want none of it. I feel that I am happier without it. I do not want to discount the future joy or sorrow,—no objection to the joy, but as prevision includes both, I prefer the curtain to remain unlifted.

I do not think spirits are prophets any more than men are prophets; but as there is a great difference in the latter in reference to prevision, so there are differences in the former. The outlook of the former may be and is better than ours, and so may be, perhaps, approximately prophetic.

I have the idea that all prevision is mathematical. The future is the product of the past. Given the factors, the unknown quantity can be made manifest, and thus the future is solved. I do not mean that the future is figured out literally; but that the principle of prevision is mathematical. There have been geniuses who, on giving them an intricate sum, requiring in the solution necessarily a great complication of figures, yet the sum total or the answer is ready on the instant. The observer, a man of figures, goes through the operation, and with much calculation finds the genius's instantaneous answer correct every time, proving a royal road to exist, but which cannot be converted into a thoroughfare.

By some such road as this the future may be known to angelic minds, or minds in the supernal; and, as I have said, sometimes this prophetic knowledge finds expression through human souls; but as yet prophecy or prevision is not a thoroughfare even for spirits generally; at least so it seems to me, and I think it best that it is so.

There may be spirits of a high order with prophetic insight, and to whom coming events are ever present; and thus the world and its environment, with its inhabitants, spirits, and mortals, is run on an intelligent basis; and though most of the previsions that leak into this mundane sphere are through dreams, premonitions, nightmares, epileptic or shattered organisms, they at least show that there is prescient and prophetic power in the universe, both beyond mortal and ordinary spiritual reach.

Does not the Concord philosopher, from whom we have quoted, give us an inkling of the idea in the lines herein quoted, and also where he says: "There is a crack in everything that God has made, and the light of heaven shines through the crevice"? I feel somewhat indebted to these "cracks" in human nature, and yet it is a blessed thing to be whole.

XXVI.

Conclusions on several interesting and important points.

I.   There is no question of the fact with me that we have invisibly around us an environment composed of spirits, who have once been mortals on earth, and that they are still interested in us.   I hardly need to say this only as a summing-up, for the reader, if he has got as far as this, will have inferred as much from the foregoing fragments of my experience.   I know of no intelligence, and can conceive of none, that does not proceed from a human organization. I do not mean the materialistic idea, that the mind is the result of the human organization, for I have learned to look upon the human organization, in a logical sense, as the product of the human spirit; but that, in a worldly point of view, the genesis of intelligence is human.   The Great First Cause is not intelligent in the sense we usually define the idea, and that any oral or written intelligence is human and not divine in its origin.

In a word, that Moses or some ancient wise man,

or the departed spirit of some man, wrote the Decalogue, and it was not by the finger of God, directly or indirectly, so that the work was not superhuman in any sense, unless one considers a spirit superhuman, which I do not; neither did the angel whom St. John was going to worship consider himself superhuman, for he said so, as recorded in the book of Revelations. The phenomena of modern Spiritualism suggests how this might have been done, and Moses have been honest; and in the suggestion how in that age there might have been good reasons for crediting it to Divinity to add to its authority. I think it possible that the Decalogue was written by a spirit, and, if so, this invisible intelligence was human, for spirits are human beings once mortal, now called immortals.

My conclusion is supplemented by the fact that the testimony of this invisible intelligence itself is that it is human. In every instance, from 1848 to date, no matter what the nature or character of the demonstration, comes the positive assurance that "I am thy brother man, and once a dweller like you upon the earth." This bottom fact, the basis of modern Spiritualism, as a statement, is as certain as the fact that there is such an *ism* current in the world. Identification of a spirit is difficult, and often a questionable matter, not so the fact that the invisible communicator is a spirit.

II. The estimate put by the great and good spirits on accumulated wealth, which is such an item

of desire here, is a low-grade one. The most disappointed man who passes over the river of death is
the man of wealth,—starting from this side as a man
of consequence, and becoming at once a nobody in
the new relation. This is not always so, and need
not be the case, but such is the general fact. I do
not expect, by saying this, to reduce the value or the
desire, or the love of, or the acquisition of, wealth. I
do not even expect to reform myself. I only know
there is danger in it that the many do not escape.
Escape, possibly, may be my compensation for the
lack of it.

I know, also, when not an idol, it is one of the
most useful adjuncts to a man's condition; or, as
Burns says : —

> "Not for to hide it in a hedge,
> Nor for a train attendant;
> But for the glorious privilege
> Of being independent!"

I am aware that but for wealth Washington would
never have been the Father of his Country, nor Theodore Parker have been the iconoclast he was if pen-
ury " had chilled the genial current of his soul," or
Wendell Phillips have had the self-denial to dodge
ambition for truth's sake but for his bank account;
still the words of Pollock fit most human cases, only
substitute the word wealth for gold in the passage
quoted : —

> "Gold, many hunted, sweat, and bled for gold;
> Waked all the night and labored all the day.
> And what was this allurement, dost thou ask?

A dust dug from the bowels of the earth,
Which, being cast into the fire, came out
A shining thing that fools admired, and called
A god; and in devout and humble plight
Before it kneeled, the greater to the less;
And at its altar sacrificed ease, peace,
Truth, faith, integrity, good conscience, friends,
Love, charity, benevolence, and all
The sweet and tender sympathies of life."

Wealth, I am aware, is a great means of civilization. The love of it, and the pursuit of it, has distanced missionary work as a civilizer. A nation must have accumulated wealth before it can have culture, and, for efficiency, it must be concentrated in a minority, not diffused. We can say of it as the ancients said of offences: "It must needs be that wealth comes, but woe unto him by whom it comes."

I do not mean that elevation of soul, heart, love, and sympathy abound with the poor, and all the selfishness with the rich. There is as much meanness, often more, in the idolatry of wealth as in its possession. There are too many exceptions to the rule for the wealthy class to have the monopoly of selfishness, yet selfishness is one of the prime factors in its production; still, it may almost be said that the possession as well as the love of wealth is the root of all evil,—that is, it is dangerous to the spirit; and modern Spiritualism, by its prevision of the next life, will yet teach mankind to a practical point that fact, so that men will not die mere money-bags; they will grow under its teachings centrifugal and diffusive, gradually investing their surplus money, not for its semi-annual dividends, but for its value in the next world. Invested here, but becoming "Summer-Land Securities" there.

III. I set a high value on phenomenal Spiritualism, or the spiritual manifestations. They may be trifles in themselves, but not trifles in their connection with unseen intelligences. They are the accented features of the subject. Practically, phenomenal Spiritualism is the whole of modern Spiritualism, or its only distinguishing feature. Modern Spiritualism defined means sensuous proof that man survives death and communicates with his fellow-men who are still living in the form.

Other *isms* claim a faith in a future life, more or less vague, as a sentiment, a hope, or a belief. Some have the idea intuitively; but most people rest on Bible revelation, or the education growing out of it. I think that both the intuitional and the vague idea have been greatly strengthened even into rational thought in church teachings by the spreading of modern Spiritualism, and without recognizing the source of the rationalizing influence. This is more noticeable at funeral ceremonies than anywhere else.

It is wholly the phenomena that make the sentiment, or hope, or belief a matter of fact. Intuitive and hopeful people take comfort, or try to in an emergency, in the expressions of holy writ, such as these, for instance: "I am the resurrection and the life;" "Because I live, ye shall live also," and other similar hopeful affirmations. Practical, or matter-of-fact men, which class includes most men of this age, say or feel otherwise, and point to "Rachel, mourning for her children, and refusing to be comforted because they are not," and say there is the fact; no glittering generalities can dry those tears, and everybody outside of Spiritualism knows that it is true.

There are some who consider phenomenal Spiritualism as light and trivial, and would consign it to a back seat, and make more prominent the ethical teachings of the subject. I am not one of such. I have been more deeply moved by a few ultra mortal raps than by any incarnated eloquence ever uttered. Not that I love education and progress less,—far from that,—but I like the phenomena more, because they, and they alone, to me have extended life and progress beyond the grave by their sensuous evidence. Shut the door on the phenomena, and the "gates" are not "ajar,"—shut that door, and you shut out the light of modern Spiritualism. If you make the subject, as it would be then, wholly ethical, it would be but one *ism* more, and be hardly a modification or an improvement upon current liberal religious thought; it would lack even the culture that has grown up in and around the earlier established orders of religious belief.

I am not forgetting inspiration, nor the influences that have almost suggested a royal road to eloquent knowledge. Without the phenomena these high-toned moments could hardly be claimed as spiritual ministrations in the modern sense; but the phenomena, admitted and recognized, then these inspirational efforts become a part of the general whole as one of the phases of the spiritual manifestations. Such inspirations and influences are as often seen in the walks of religious life as they are in the walks of Spiritualism. The Spiritualist knows from his experience that a law exists for it, and the light shines through the thin places or cracks in the curtain between the two worlds whether the thin places or the cracks know it or not.

IV. Spirits, I think, have a way of reaching us directly. I think the influences of our own spirit friends are more reliably from them when they come directly to us than when they come through a third party. I am getting to think that one's own impressions are as liable to be spiritual impressions as to be our own impressions. I have no doubt that spirits near us by love, relationship, or affinity reach our sensorium as readily as we do ourselves in our normal genesis of thought.

Science, as Dr. Storrs says, has not bridged the chasm between molecular action and human thought, and neither have we ourselves, nor even individually for ourselves, bridged it. We know, if our attention has been called to it, and have noticed the process that our emotions of affection and our intuitions seem to have a deeper root in our consciousness or our being than our intellect has. We examine our thoughts, the product of our mind, as a something a little outside of ourselves, as it were, semi-objectively,

—not so our emotions or intuitions. I have an idea that spirits *en rapport* with us have their avenue of communication in that deeper department of our being, and with us know and read our train or flow of thought that we call our intellectual life.

We do not know the source of sudden thoughts or ideas that seem to bolt into our minds; they may be self-induced, they may sprout into consciousness spontaneously, and they may be the influences or silent whisperings of the spirits. It is difficult to tell in the mental dynamics of our being what is our own, and what is from the "divinity that shapes our ends" or our own thoughts. This is a very apt expression for what is now known as "spiritual influences," and leads us to think that Shakespeare was a medium, and very sensitive to the influences of the spirit world. Certainly Shakespeare, the man, and Shakespeare, the genius, were very different people, and impressed people differently, or we would today have known as much of him as we do of his contemporary, Francis Bacon.

V. A bright young spirit, very mature, however, in wisdom, gave a message,—it may have been allegorical, probably was. I will try and put it briefly into an intelligible form, thus: "I love my medium, and she wants some dollars for her uses, and I want some dollars, too, for myself." He got the dollars, no matter how; here is what he, the spirit, says: "I tried various ways for the possession of what I wanted; I offered my dollars in exchange, but no spirit wanted them. They wanted love, truth, sympathy, wisdom, and for any of these they had returns to make of what I wanted; but dollars nobody wanted, and, as you mortals would say, I have, in these dollars, an elephant on my hands, and I do not know what to do with it or them." This interview was quite interesting; I have tried to give the substance of it in these few words. It suggested some ideas on the subject of wealth from a spirit's standpoint. I will try to present my ideas, using that abridged message as an influence.

Many people struggling under difficulties, and against odds, wonder why the spirits who loved them, and aided them when in the form, do not do so now when out of the form. It certainly would be an easier thing to do, it would seem, than it is to materialize a form, as they often do. Spirits certainly take an interest in us, and would naturally, one would think, be happy or unhappy, as we are happy or unhappy. They must be very much changed, fundamentally, if they are not. I am very sure, did they not see some "glorious beaming star too far over yon mountain's hight" for mortal vision, they would be.

It is very evident that the soft and wealthy conditions of this life do not come to the most deserving; rather the reverse, it would seem to me. Strip from the wealthy their accumulations, they would hardly hold their own by the side of those more or less stripped by the chances and circumstances of life, as lovable, sympathetic people. When they are thus stripped, as all will be in the undress of the spirit, when this "mortal coil is shuffled off," there will be a regrading of souls, and very different from the current one of earthly life. It will not be surprising then if many of the first will be last, and many of the last will be first,— many a millionaire be a street-sweeper, and many a man of mean estate here will be clothed in purple and fine linen there.

I think in a world where wealth is goodness, spirituality, thought, wisdom, and the like, that the denizens of it in reaching their friends, who are still in the form, have lost their estimate of our wealth that is so appreciated here on earth, and of no value there. We who are adults have seen children play with marbles with all the earnestness of business life, as if marbles for the time being was their all in all, happy in possession, quarreling even for their accumulation; and we looking on can hardly realize the value of what they are aiming at and making such a fuss about, except by remembering we were all children once, and had marbles ourselves. It seems to me that spirits have about the same idea of wealth as we adults have of the marbles and foibles of our youth; we have got past them. Thus the Goulds, Vanderbilts, Astors, Sages, Fields, etc., are simply children who have great accumulations of marbles through luck and skill, and we, or rather the spirits, can simply wonder what they will do with them when they are done playing.

I am not forgetting the influence and bearing that wealth may have on one's soul or mental being. I am not forgetting the independence of thought that affluence sometimes gives its possessor. I know many men who have been brave in expression beyond their fellows, who would not have been thus leaders of thought but for their inherited or acquired wealth. True, there are exceptions; let not the "money-bags" of life flatter themselves that these exceptions are the rule; for, as a whole, wealth narrows most men, or else the quality of narrowness,— caution, cold-bloodedness, selfishness, are combined more or less with the luck or parsimony which have been the factors of such accumulation. It is better to have hope without wealth than to have wealth without hope; better still to have both. There is much truth in the orphic saying of Emerson: "A man takes from his soul what he puts into his money-chest."

XXVII.

THE BOSTON OUTLOOK.

Thoughts that the locality suggests to a Spiritualist.

I think the Spiritualists who live in, especially if they are natives of, Boston have good reasons for being proud of their locality. I do not mean that it is of the " burning bush " order,— a place to put off one's shoes, because of its being holy ground,—for a good deal of its *terra firma* is artificial; but I do not count that as in any sense unholy, for that has been ‧ a decided improvement upon the original first out-line of it as nature made it, or God, if one likes that expression better.

Part of this artificial addition, a very small part, to be sure, has been selected by a liberal Spiritualist and dedicated to the spirit world, and a spiritual temple erected thereon, and yet, with that creditable event in my mind, I am not proud of Boston for any special holiness, and so what I am going to say I do so with my "shoes" on, uninfluenced by the Horebic injunction. I was saying, we Spiritualists who live in Boston have many reasons to be proud of it. It is a bright and respectable old place for a new country, or new to Caucassian life, as America is. In one of Plutarch's records of "Ancient Lives," a man says: "I thank the gods that I am a man and not a woman, a freeman and not a slave, a Greek and not a barbarian." Never having been a woman, I cannot say as the Grecian did; one, also, is not very sure how free he is or how enslaved, and so, also, would I be careful how I look down upon the barbarian, for such are as liable to be in our very midst as on, or beyond, the frontiers; still the Grecian's remark is an analogous one to my expression of pride in being a Bostonian.

I am aware Boston would have been Boston without my aid, or the aid of three or four ancestral generations who may have been an atom or two in it from its earlier days. I am aware, also, that all over this broad land are the sons and daughters of this "Hub," as it is sometimes called, who have as much inherent right to be proud of it as I have; so, while I express my pride in being thus generically connected with the locality, I do not put on any airs, or prevent any distant ones from having their pride in this or any other place on the world's map.

I have something to say about Boston, and I may get it said after awhile. By Boston I do not mean the little peninsular on the coast of the Bay State of two or three square miles of land, which the Indians called Shawmut, nor it with the accretions of territory, of which I have spoken, by the "removal of mountains" in the neighborhood and casting them into the sea, thus doubling or trebling its area; nor it with the supplements of contiguous cities and towns by annexation, so that now, geographically speaking, it has a territory over ten times what it had when it first became a figure in history. I include its vicinity, or the general indefinite locality which goes to make up the intellectual atmosphere of this still small, but may I not say rather brilliant, spot in the world of letters and of thought.

To having any claim of fanciful fitness to being the "Hub of the Universe," we have got to include Concord, with its past and living lights, and Harvard College, and other objects, going by other names; and then we must remember the universe includes some undiscovered country outside of earth, — and, any way, it is an awful strain to call it the "Hub," and yet who does not know what is meant when the "Hub" is spoken of? But with all these qualifications and reductions, it seems to me to be more of a "Hub" than any spot of which I can think. So, though I do not consider it a "Hub," or call it one, I always consider the appellation complimentary, whether intended so or not.

Historically, politically, religiously, learnedly, financially, socially, this Boston, in its enlarged sense, has much to its credit, and, of course, some to its debit or discredit, but the balance is very large on its credit side, its enemies, if it has any, will admit that. Of course, many people, — people that are not only proud of this city, but people that this city is proud of, and who, by their learning and their reputation or influence have helped to make it the

conspicuity it is, and who will agree to all I have
said as yet, but will not go with me now in saying
that one of the things that helps make me proud
of this locality, that enhances its value to me, is the
reception it gives to modern Spiritualism.

How many pleasant or intelligent faces will fall a
shade or two on such an intimation as this; without
any basis of truth such will of course think, and are
happy in knowing, that it is not true, and, if it was,
it would be retrogression and a stain rather than the
source of pride to anyone. They might be charitable,
perhaps, to the writer, and suppose him to be living
in his little world and meeting Spiritualists only, and
if meeting others not counting them. he has mistaken
the extent,— strabismus is in his eye, and he thinks
the world squints, as our aunt Nancy, at the North
End, once said, whose husband was a Millerite, and
I was laughing at her for such notions, when she
replied : "Only think of it, how many do believe it.
I hardly see a person who does not believe it, and is
not preparing for it." Well, I suppose we all do see
things pretty much as we wish to, or as our interest
dictates.

Still, it pleases me to feel that I am right, and
proud of even being proud of the fact as something
of a feature of the locality at the present time.
Modern Spiritualism started, as we all know, in a
small way, in the western part of the State of New
York, less than two score years ago, and has spread
now all over the world ; at least, in every part of the
civilized and the uncivilized world, also, are found its

adherents, and the practical working of the law that is fundamental in its teachings, and its believers, now running into the millions, and has already become one of the large sects of the world (using "sects" as a general term of division in religious thought), having a literature also of no mean pretension, and publications, magazines, and newspapers in a dozen different languages.

In thus spreading itself more or less all over the world, it seems to me to have found a congenial atmosphere in this vicinity. I am aware there is no place anywhere that can be called its special center. But where is there more of it concentrated than is the case here? which seems to make it almost a duty to notice the fact before finishing this book, and which I am now doing. Look at the meetings for spiritualistic teachings that this locality sustains. See the number of mediums that dispense the idea in sittings or seances, in tests, messages, healing, and other ways, and by other names sometimes; and with regard to the more sensuous phenomena there seems to be in this city about all the time a dozen mediums for materialization, to say nothing about other physical phenomena. The manifestations for teachings and for tests also, in a private way, are enjoyed in all parts of the city, even in the higher walks of social life that the world knows but little about. This, to some extent, is so everywhere both in this country and England and on the continent, but it is remarkably so in this vicinity of which I am now speaking.

Speakers and believers all over the country look fondly to this city for the rising thought, as if it were the home of this "Dawning Light," and the prestige of this locality often endorses the utterances of unknown persons. Thoughts acceptable here are apt from that fact to be acceptable elsewhere, and thus the push or the Boston momentum is felt at a great distance, and almost everywhere.

The fact that the first spiritual temple, of which we have before spoken, is blossoming out here in its fine architectural proportions, is but one of the pointers that show in thus owning up of my pride in this locality that I am not drawing on my imagination for my facts.

I once heard the Rev. Nehemiah Adams, as he had just returned from the death-bed scene of a very pious member of his church, relate the circumstance at a large meeting then being held in Tremont Temple. It is too long a story to relate here; but it was about the seeing of a spirit that he, the dying man, knew when a mortal; and the circumstances were such, and the prophecy that had been suggested by the manifestation was of such a character, that it proved there was no decay of mentality as the life of that man was closing in. But to Mr. Adams, his pastor, instead of this being a natural fact, it was looked upon and spoken of as a divine one,—an angel had manifested to this brother on account of his great and manifested piety.

The reverend gentleman remarked after narrating the circumstances: "The curtain between the two

worlds was thinner than it once was." I have no
doubt of that fact myself; but where was his authority,
outside of modern Spiritualism, for saying so? The
thought suggested to me by the remark was whether
there were not, and always had been "thin places"
on this earth,—places more open to spiritual influences than other parts of the earth's surface.

As in the human organization there are ganglionic
centers or spots, or sensitive places, which are not
universal in the human system, so there may be, so
to speak, ganglionic spots or centers on the earth's
surface. Of course it is likely to be as much or more
in the race living on the spot as in the location; but
may be that is not so certain. It would seem as if
Palestine, Greece, Rome and Egypt, and, later, Brit-
ain and many other places, suggest such an idea which
has had so much to do with human history.

Palestine, for instance, only about as large, and as
unattractive as Wales, has left its mark deeply on
the human race, giving the civilized world its religion,
and Phœnicia, almost a part of it, the alphabet.
Why did it happen so on that circumscribed and
unattractive spot, when there were so many superior
ones in every respect? It is said that Frederick II.
was sent to Syria against his will; the church perse-
cuted him, and one of the charges was his saying
that, "If God had ever seen Naples, he never would
have selected Palestine for his chosen people." I
quote this circumstance to show it is not the attractive features of a locality that make it one of these
ganglionic or "thin places." Neither dare I say that

•

Boston is any more ganglionic, or thin, or sensitive, or magnetic than many other spots in the American domain; only I have uttered a thought indigenous, one may say, to a " Hubite," and I must try to make it reasonable. I do not seem to have any inclination to write on an ethnological subject, and I do not know as I am capable of doing so in an interesting manner if I had; only in this closing chapter, as this city in its elastic or enlarged sense seems to be opening itself to our thought, the fact pleases me, and I felt like saying so, wondering also why it has relatively grown into such a marked locality for modern Spiritualism.

The careful reader of the preceding chapters of this book will have very easily got the author's *rationale* of the fact just stated, that it is such a marked locality, and that naturally is his belief in the basic truth that modern Spiritualism teaches, viz., that there is an intelligent spiritual environment, which means practically both a general and a special supervision of the affairs of mundane life by the spirit world. That such supervising spirits saw a tendency, or, using spiritualistic parlance, finding conditions right, have influenced one to the point which by these remarks seems to have been reached in the present modern spiritual aspect in this vicinity.

I hope there will be no solstice or retrogression in the movement, and the, so to speak, Horebic character of this locality be permanent, now having been ornamented or marked by the erection of the first spiritual temple of attractive magnitude, and dedicated to the spirits, as it should be, it having been inspired from that source; so, having said I was proud of being a Bostonian, and giving at length my reasons for being so, I hope the feeling will be permanent and enduring, and the time come, as its teachings become more and more understood, when all the people will be like-minded, proud of this locality for its sake, and rejoice in the spread of this light which has begun to shine in the world, and brightens as it continues. The city of Boston has quite a history for a spot not yet three centuries old; has been the mother also of many other places, and, as we have said, is quite a conspicuity,—far larger, in an ideal or transcendental sense, than are thousands of places of greater geographical extent. It seems, then, to be a fitting place for Spiritualism to have got a decided impetus, as it manifestly has, and if celebrated already for many things, it will be even more so for this dawning light when its truth has got implanted in the general mind, as will certainly be the case if it be a truth. I am writing as if it was, because I have solid reasons for knowing it to be so.

Seems to me if any modern "Jacob" should have a dream, here would be his pillar or bethel, where he would see the ladder reaching Heaven with the angels ascending and descending thereon, except that the Bible, and modern Spiritualism especially, teaches that not in this mountain nor in Jerusalem, nor even in Boston, is there any deific or angelic exclusiveness; but the first round of that ladder rests wherever there is a truth-loving human being.

Coleridge, translating the poetry of Schiller, makes it read thus,— it is not a literal truth, but seems to be a suggestive one, so I use it as a terminus to this chapter :—

> " The spirits' ladder,
> That from this gross and visible world of dust,
> Even to the starry world with thousand rounds,
> Builds itself up, on which the unseen powers
> Move up and down on heavenly ministries,—
> These see the glance, the unsealed eye,
> Of Jupiter's glad children born in luster."

THEODORE PARKER.

The earth is marked in many places
  With rocky scratches and furrows deep;
Boulders huge have left their traces,
  As diamond-pointed icebergs slowly creep.

Records, or scriptures, writ on stone,
  Humanity is fast translating,—
Reads wisdom from the Great Unknown,
  And grows religious speculating.

So the moral world has "boulder scratches,"
  Made by heroic souls in passing through it;
Prophets and poets,— "bearers of despatches,"—
  Lights in a world that hardly knew it.

History, rich in storied names now dead,
  None brighter shine than that great teacher;
Today is brighter for the light he shed, —
  The world still needs just such a preacher.

The "boulder scratch" of Theodore Parker,—
  Oh, who would now that mark efface? —
Put out his light, and make it darker,
  Whose transit was a blessing to the race?

His life, in years, how short it seems?
  How long in manly work for human good!
Religion in him was life,— not dreams;
  Mute are his foes; his mission understood.

The voice of bigotry now is hushed
  That called him heretic, though sent of God;
Full many a sham by him lies crushed,
  And others safely walk where he in peril trod.

www.ingramcontent.com/pod-product-compliance
Lightning Source LLC
Chambersburg PA
CBHW020902020726
47497CB00005B/1514